SHORELINE OF INFINITY

science fiction magazine
...otland for the Universe

CW00828748

ISSUE 34:
SPRING 2023

ISSN: 2059-2590
ISBN: 978-1-7396736-8-0

Submissions of fiction, art, reviews, poetry, non-fiction are welcomed: visit the website to find out how to submit

www.shorelineofinfinity.com

Publisher
Shoreline of Infinity Publications /
The New Curiosity Shop
Edinburgh
Scotland

070323

Co-founder:
Noel Chidwick

Co-founder:
Mark Toner

Deputy Editor
Poetry Editor:
Russell Jones

Fiction Editor:
Eris Young

Reviews Editor:
Ann Landman

Non-fiction Editor:
Pippa Goldschmidt

Marketing &
Publicity Editor,
Proof Reader:
Yasmin Kanaan

Production Editor:
James T. Harding

Copy-editors:
Pippa Goldschmidt
Russell Jones
Iain Maloney
Eris Young
Cat Hellisen

Fiction Consultant:
Eric Brown

EDITORIAL TEAM

CONTENTS

COVER ART
Ross MacRae
Instagram: @ross.macrae.art

FIRST CONTACT
www.shorelineofinfinity.com
contact@shorelineofinfinity.com
Twitter: @shoreinf

PULL UP A LOG

How have I found myself writing *Shoreline of Infinity*'s first editorial of 2023?!

When I initially got involved with the magazine back in 2019, with a weird little 1,000-word story featured in Issue 14, I never thought I'd one day be sitting here, contemplating how to introduce a new issue.

I'm thrilled with the stories and voices we have the privilege of featuring in number 34, from brilliant writers in Scotland and beyond. There are stories populated with sprout-children, alien wolves and murderous cleaner-bots, poetry that brings the ineffably human into outer space, as well as speculative nonfiction wondering what will emerge once the structures we've built collapse.

I couldn't be more grateful to Mark and Noel for giving me the chance to work with them. But even more, I am grateful to them for simply founding an excellent magazine, and for their tireless commitment to science fiction, both in Scotland and beyond.

I'm well aware of what a heavy mantle myself and the rest of the core team of Pippa, Russell and Ann have taken on – four of us to replace just two founders! And we're determined to do the magazine justice, celebrating the history of Scottish science fiction while looking towards the future, not only to what Scottish SF might look like ten or fifty years from now, but how it might continue to reflect the changing landscape of the genre, and continue to be in dialogue with the issues facing all of us right now.

And as we put the finishing touches on Issue 34, and spring gently starts to poke its nose out of the ground, I find myself looking forward to new beginnings, new stories, new friends and new horizons for *Shoreline* in 2023.

– Eris Young

Wolf Teeth

L. R. Lam

A wind age, a wolf age –
before the world goes headlong.
No man will have
mercy on another.
— *Völuspá, 10th century Old Norse Poem*

The wolves came from the sky.

Though they yearned to howl, to shriek and stop this strange world in its tracks, they dampened their screams. Their leaders had grander plans first, and the wolves were not needed. Not yet.

They waited. The wolves prowled, sticking to the shadows throughout the world. When they could, the wolves picked off their prey, one by one, freezing them with one sharp burst of echolocation that stopped the creatures in their tracks. These puny aliens, with dull teeth, no claws, skin soft as overripe fruit. The wolves tore into meat, drank blood, crunched bones, lapping up the marrow. They waited for their next orders. On a clear night, the wolves could raise their four eyes and just barely make out the twinkle of that far away star, through the swirls of the waves of light these creatures they hunted could not see.

Art: Simon Walpole

The world was dead and dying. The creatures' dens no longer lit with heatless light. Their machines no longer whirred through the sky, over the sea, or along the paths they'd eked through the land.

At last, it was time. As one, the wolves lifted their muzzles and howled. The packs descended, no longer hiding in the darkness. They ate, they burrowed deep in their dens. They slept, bellies full, before they hunted again. Wolves did not dream. It was not for the wolves to question what the leader of their pack, on that faraway star, told them to.

They hunted. They feasted. They mated. They slept. It would not take long now. The wolves' teeth were sharp.

Outgoing missive:
Location: 55.948595, -3.199913
Date: 04.01.2029
Is there anyone out there? Anyone at all?
Please answer.
Please.

— Jotunheimen National Park, Norway, 2030

Einar wasn't sure if he was alive or not.

He lay in snow stained pink with blood. All was silent, as ever. Einar must move, but terror kept him still, his breath coming in shallow gasps. He wouldn't hear the wolf's footsteps through the snow, or catch the growling deep in its throat. It would be hot breath against his neck, the fetid smell of old blood, and then sharp death and darkness.

He could not freeze to death. Pushing himself up, he brushed snowflakes from his cheeks and looked around. No wolf crouched behind him.

Hating having his sense of touch dampened, Einar wriggled his fingers in his thick gloves until the blood flowed. He pressed his stiff hands against the gash in his side, slowing the sluggish bleeding. He dragged himself to his knees.

His uncle's body sprawled before him. His torso had been ripped open, dark pink snow already piled in his gaping abdomen.

Einar's mouth opened, his throat closed. The wind rose, biting his face. He bowed his head, and his tears froze on his eyelashes. The grief was as sharp as the gash in his side, shock numbing the edges.

His uncle. His *uncle*.

Einar was too weak to bring his uncle's body back for a proper *likferd*. He would not be able to watch over him, even for the one night they spared rather than the traditional eight. He could not be absent from the hunt.

If Einar did not move soon, he would never make it back.

He crawled over the snow and closed his uncle's open eyes, hands dancing as he signed both a quick prayer and the words to one of the funeral songs. Memories flashed behind his eyelids, but he forced them down.

Grieve later.

Wasting precious time, Einar found a loose fir branch and, grunting with pain, laid it over his uncle's face. Not a proper burial, not even close, yet better than nothing at all.

The Vargrs' dark blue blood tainted the snow. Nothing remained of the two wolves but a tuft of their ice-blue fur, the splash of indigo blood, and their tracks in the snow.

One wolf, the one with a jagged scar on its flank, had grasped him in its extra forearms, horribly human, the pointed talons digging into his shoulders. He had not heard the wolf's keening, paralysing call; he was deaf, so he never could. The wolf's mouth had opened wide, its fetid breath warm against his face, and Einar thought those pointed teeth would be the last thing he ever saw.

Einar's ski bike was still stashed in the trees, right next to his uncle's. Tears froze on his cheeks again. He went through the motions – turning on the small heater, smooth as a river stone and glowing like a coal, and sliding it into the pouch within his parka to keep him warm. He made sure the pack was tied securely to the bike.

He sat on the bike, unable to start. He crouched around the warm stone, letting out a cry that he could not hear.

The wolf named Riv watched the human cub from the trees. Saliva dripped from his mouth. He'd killed one human. The hunter that had killed Riv's littermate. The meat had been warm and good, his first kill in almost a week. Blood and muscle, bone and marrow. He wanted to return to his den, bringing the last of the meat to share with the rest of the pack, then to sleep with his mates and cubs in a pile of fur, soft breathing, and heartbeats. He should kill the young human cub. It would be so easy. The cub was keening with loss. Riv knew that emotion, disliked that it made him pause.

The cub was prey. The cub should be eaten like the others, to feed his young and his mates. The wolves would make this world their own until the leader of the pack arrived from the stars and sent them to the next world. Snow bit into the pads of his paws. He crouched down, paws cracking the ice below the snow. The wolf's second pair of eyes saw the pulsing of blood, the warmth emanating from skin. Riv could smell the human cub. Sweat, fear, and that tantalising scent of prey.

The boy started his noisy machine and made his way up the mountain, too fast for Riv to follow. He would not waste the energy. He would take this meat to his family. His first family. His new family. His proof that he himself was no longer a cub, but a wolf.

Turning his head, his muzzle snuffled the pine and ice-scented wind, and his ears sang with the call from other members of his pack. They had finally breached the home of the humans on this mountain. They feasted and called for their brethren to join them.

Riv buried his catch, hoping to return later. For now, perhaps he could bring his cubs fresher, warmer meat.

By the time he reached Ulvefort, Einar was barely conscious. His breath hitched in his chest, the cold deep in his bones despite the heater. Soft snowflakes fell from the sky, resting on his shoulders, his hat, his eyelashes.

The metal and pine gates gaped open. Einar did not wish to enter. He knew, with every heavy step he took towards his home, that even if he could hear, there would only be silence.

The bodies were gone, taken by the wolves. Only dark red splotches showed where they had fallen. Who did they belong to? Lukas? Askel? Gull? One of those spots of blood could belong to his Mor. If he lost both his uncle and his mother in one day…

Einar's breath misted in the cold air as he swayed on his feet. He knew he was in shock, dizzy from blood loss, frostbite nipping at his fingers. His mouth opened and he let out a low moan he felt reverberate deep within his chest.

A door to one of the barracks opened. A white, frightened face poked her head out.

"Einar!" she signed.

Einar touched the side of his nose: "Mor."

He collapsed as soon as he crossed the threshold.

KILLER WOLVES FROM SPACE
Article for Vakten, 16 December 2029. 10.30 am.
By Dr Inge Tveit

Such a ridiculous-sounding headline. It sounds like something from one of those rags you'd buy in line at the store. Bat Boy seen. Hunters shoot an angel. Politicians and royalty are secretly robots or lizards – that always seemed more likely than the others. Yet here we are, cowering from killer wolves from outer space.

The short version is: this isn't good. Some are calling these creatures the Vargr, after the wolves in Ragnarök. They first descended in Norway, as far as we can tell, but within a few days, they were everywhere. We are living in the end times, so many say. We don't even know how many will still be able to access this article.

I am a zoologist, and my speciality is wolves. I also had a passing interest in cryptozoology, more out of fascination than true belief. Little did I know how completely and utterly these interests would collide.

My team managed to capture one of the wolves. We cryogenically froze it before the blood became too acidic and it decomposed at the accelerated rate of other specimens. Vakten has asked me to break it down into layman's terms for the public.

They do, at first glance, look like wolves, though three times as large. They have fur that changes depending on their local climate. In Norway, they are ice-blue, thick and warm as a polar bear's fur. In the deserts, they shed nearly all of their fur, leaving only a short stubble, and it turns a sandy brown. They have three rows of pointed teeth. They have four eyes, and the extra set can sense infared and therefore see in the dark. Their snouts are shorter than a wolf's and have two extra nostrils. A wolf can smell one hundred times better than a German Shepherd. A Vargr can smell better than a wolf. They have four main limbs, but vestigial extra forearms with human-like hands, prehensile, tipped with black claws that release a paralytic.

Their main form of hunting is echolocation, far more sophisticated than bats or whales. They can hit a frequency that pierces animal ears. Anyone who has heard the call and lived – not many – have said it feels like having knives plunged into their ears.

In short, they are like something deliberately engineered to be our worst nightmare.

These Vargr are difficult to kill. Bullets slow them down, but rarely stop them. They are immune to all poisons tried so far. They breed quickly, and already there is roughly one wolf on Earth for every three humans.

I wish I could end this on a hopeful note. I don't think I can. Like the rest of the world, I pray.

Riv had eaten well. His belly was full. His pack curled around him, dreaming of the hunt. His new mate, Yilva, stretched next to him, exposing her belly so their sleepy pups could suckle. He should be sleeping. He should be content.

There were not many humans left in this part of the world. They would have to leave, to go further down the mountain, finding pockets of prey hidden in the crevices of the land. Riv did admire these aliens' tenacity. They had been the hunters of this world, tamed the wilderness and the stronger creatures of the forest, the tundra, the jungle. It made the hunt all the sweeter.

He shouldn't have let the pup escape. Even if the human cub could not hear Riv's call, he could easily have taken the boy in his jaws. He'd stood over the young creature after he'd killed the older human.

Yilva had hurt herself in the scuffle and gone back to the den to nurse her wounds and see to their cubs. Their pack had been bigger, but the human hunters had killed several, leaving only the betas, Fiavin and Pirin, and the new alpha, Nivvag.

Instead, the wolf had watched the cub, thinking he looked so small. Wolves grew quickly – from cub to hunter in just three months. These puny humans took years before they became hunters, yet this small boy – older than Riv – had killed many wolves already.

Without knowing why, he had turned, leaving the steaming meat and the child, and watched from the trees as the boy awoke and grieved.

He'd never gone back for the meat of the other man. Instead, he had answered the call of his alpha. By the time he arrived, the fight was over, the wolves fleeing with their prey. Riv had grabbed a human in his jaws and carried it back to his den. A kill he hadn't even made. The meat had tasted sour.

Riv stretched out, moving the fingers of his extra forearms in the darkness, waiting for sleep that did not come.

Out of a settlement of six hundred and seventeen souls, only two hundred and ninety-two remained. Most of the other hunters were lost in the fight. The Vargr must have recognised their scent, and the hunters were the first line of defence.

Ulvefort fixed the gate. They shovelled away the blood-soaked snow. They had funerals in the church for the departed. They drilled into the ground. The survivors wondered why they, too, had not been eaten. Einar's wound healed into a scab and then the beginnings of a scar. Frostbite claimed none of his fingers or toes.

The attack was his fault. He must have been sloppy, left too many trails, and the wolves had followed him home. He kept searching the old archive logs of the internet as he often did, piecing together fragments from the past. A cry for help from Edinburgh that he could not answer. An article about the wolves' physiology. Old Norse poems and the tales of the wolves of Ragnarök.

Einar and his uncle had been the best hunters in the settlement. Einar's immunity to the Vargrs' high-pitched keening howl had saved both of their lives countless times. Einar once asked his uncle what the cry sounded like, and his uncle had told him the tale of the banshee and her shrieking call.

"The sound blocks out the world. It's like closing your eyes tight when you're sitting close to the fire," he'd said. 'Everything is gone, but you know the heat and danger is lurking behind your eyelids.'

The wolves came from the sky when Einar was four years old. He didn't know what life was like before, though his family told him stories. His Onkel Halvard especially loved to weave tales on the long, bitter nights in winter. Those memories were like shards of glass in his mind. He picked them up and the grief cut him deep.

He and his uncle used to sit outside, bundled in furs, his uncle's voice lulling Einar into a half-sleep as they watched the stars and the Aurora Borealis glimmering overhead. Halvard told him of sprawling cities with millions of souls. Technology that was not constantly patched and failing. Einar had hearing aids as a child, but they'd broken eight years ago. Sometimes Einar thought his uncle must have exaggerated – surely humans couldn't have once flown above the clouds in great hulking machines of metal. Surely they couldn't have gone to the moon?

This far up the mountain was supposed to be safe. Here was where they were meant to survive the Ragnarok.

Einar shivered as the dark nights continued to pass, growing colder as winter crept closer. The sun soon never rose above the mountains, lending only a thin, pink light to the sky for a few hours before fleeing again. The snowfall turned to a blizzard, temperatures cemented well below freezing. Rations were plentiful, but only because they were meant to be feeding more mouths. Sentries patrolled the walls. Now the Vargr knew where the settlement was, Einar watched the lips of the people of Ulvefort as they whispered, it was only a matter of time before the monsters returned to finish what they started.

When the blizzard passed, Einar gathered together his hunting gear. The spear gun, dipped in a poison made from juniper berries that weakened the Vargr. His uncle and Einar had discovered this by accident. A dart gun, ammunition similarly treated. A knife. The tracker that would vibrate if it picked up the heat signature of a Vargr. His tent and sleeping roll. His personal heater. Food and water. Scent disguiser. Extra fuel for his ski bike. Night vision and normal binoculars, and the Ulvefort alarm that he hoped would never vibrate again.

His mother watched him pack it all, her face creased in anxiety.

"Don't do this," she signed after tapping him on the shoulder for his attention. "The ice has been too thick. They won't return until spring. That gives us time for a plan."

"We don't know they'll wait until spring. That gives them time to formulate a plan too," he signed back.

She bowed her head. He touched her gently below the chin, forcing her to look at him.

"I have to do this, Mor. I can't sit here, knowing that if I had been stronger that day, I could have saved Onkel Halvard. The wolves wouldn't have found you."

"Think of all the attacks you prevented over the years."

"Not enough. Mor." His signs grew more agitated. "Let me do this. I have to do it for Onkel, for everyone we lost. For me."

"I can't lose you, too."

There was nothing to say. Feeling so much older than seventeen, he rested his forehead against hers before pulling back and turning away.

```
"Unidentified flying object, do you read? This is
the United States Air Force. You are in a no-fly
zone. Do you copy?"

[transcriber note: static]

"I repeat, do you copy?"

[more static]

"General, what is our course of action?"

"Open fire."

[sound of gunfire and illegible shouting]

"General, the craft is absorbing all our
weaponry. Course of action?"
```

[more gunfire]

"Pray."

   - Transcript of audio from Cannon Air Force Base,
      New Mexico, the first place of attack in the
         United States, 06.19.2028, 20:50 hours.

The pups sickened first. They turned away from their mothers' dugs. They grew hot with fever. The adults exchanged worried whirrs and clicks.

Riv had thought they had more time.

The Désir, the leaders of all the wolf packs, had programmed the wolves to hunt. For each new planet, they would tinker with the formula, make them ideal killers in their new environments against their myriad prey. They would be reborn into new bodies. They weren't meant to remember what happened before and what would happen again. Riv remembered.

When the native creatures of a world were nearly destroyed, the wolves sickened. Riv had found the logs in their craft, spending years learning Désir script. It had not been a surprise. Deep in their half-formed ancestral memories, all wolves knew that when they reached the end of the hunt, it was the end for them as well.

They thought they had more time.

Riv watched his pups die. His mates. All members of his pack. They staggered out into the cold, one by one, to find their own cairns of snow. Riv waited for his own body to sicken, to weaken, to burn. By default, he became the alpha of a pack of one. Feverishly, he used the last of his time to learn, tearing through the logs, desperation fuelling him even though it felt worthless.

Each day could be his last. He went out and caught smaller prey. Rabbits, deer. Easy prey, boring meat. Sustenance but little else.

Sometimes he wondered if he should go out into the snow, lie down and let the cold take him before the sickness could.

Yet he was a hunter. A warrior. Even if his pack was only himself now, he could not betray it.

He hunted. He waited. He turned his head to look up the

mountain, to the small, stubborn settlement of humans. The wolf's lips pulled back in a snarl.

It was never easy to track the Vargr in the snow.

Einar threaded his way through the forest, leaving his ski bike behind as soon as he reached the trees.

The fir forest was dark, the branches almost black against the pale snow. The air was so cold it seemed a heavy presence in his lungs. All smelled of pine, ice, and the slow and slumbering earth.

It took three days before he found signs of Vargr – tracks in the snow, tufts of pale fur caught in the tree bark. He came across a corpse, frozen solid, too cold for the acid in their blood to break the body down.

Einar shot the corpse. It felt good.

Einar passed the spot where his uncle had died. There was no evidence of the body. No *likferd* for his kin. He signed another prayer, then carried on.

When his uncle and Einar had been attacked, they had been searching for the den. If the wolves were all killed at once, the mountain would be safe. Einar had a good guess where the den would be. Finally, he found it. A small cave in a jagged outcrop of the mountain, half-hidden by the pines.

Einar camped in a tree that night, climbing up as far as he dared. He slept curled around his heater, his face bundled so only his eyes showed. He wedged the spear gun between his body and the tree trunk, gripping the heat tracker in his hand. He slept fitfully, jerking awake every few minutes, certain he'd felt the tracker vibrate only to find it quiet in his hand.

Hunting was lonely without his uncle. He kept looking for him as he trekked through the snow, a half-smile freezing on his face like an icicle when he realised his uncle was not there, and would never hunt with him again.

The wolves hadn't returned to their den. He wanted to see their ice-blue pelts, to pick up the spear-gun and shoot them right between the eyes. He would kill them all, from the smallest pup to that mean bastard with the scar on his flank.

Einar shifted in the branches, his leg muscles aching. From

his perch, he could barely make out the dim opening to the den. He wondered what lay inside. The gnawed bones of his friends and family. Horrible pups that would grow into killers. A place of nightmares and death.

The pale winter sunlight fled as night closed on the forest. The Vargr saw better than Einar did in the dark, and their call also served as crude echolocation. Wolves mixed with bats with creepy human arms. Living nightmares.

Einar tried to make himself comfortable, nibbling on reindeer jerky from his backpack. He spread more scent protection on himself. Even if he was downwind, he should be safe. He gripped his gun, fighting exhaustion.

The heat tracker vibrated in his hand. For a second, all Einar could do was look at it and know there was no turning back. He would kill the wolves or die trying. He hefted his spear gun.

There.

The wolf appeared like a shadow, cresting the hill. At the creature's approach, the entrance to the den glowed a brighter blue. Einar aimed the gun.

His first shot missed, burying deep in the trunk of a tree. The wolf slunk through the trees, smooth as water in a stream. Einar slotted another spear into the gun, aiming again.

The Vargr opened its jaws, releasing its paralysing howl that Einar could not hear. He shot again, narrowly missing the wolf.

Einar re-loaded, his heart hammering in his chest. His uncle had told him the howl of the wolf was so loud that other Vargr from miles away could hear and come running at impossible speeds. He could be surrounded within minutes.

The wolf turned to face him, glowing blue eyes staring into Einar's brown ones. Einar hesitated, hating himself for doing so. It was the wolf with the scarred side, the one who had given Einar a scar of his own but left him alive.

Einar let the spear fly and the wolf dodged again, the bolt lost in the snow banks. The wolf didn't howl again, as if he knew it wouldn't work. Einar loaded again, his half-frozen fingers fumbling in the dark.

The Vargr came closer, ducking his head and barrelling into

the tree. The branches shook and Einar had to reach out and clasp the trunk or fall into the snow and the wolf's waiting jaws. His spear gun tumbled from his hands, catching on the alarm around his wrist. Both fell into the white below.

Einar could not warn Ulvefort. He cursed himself for a fool. He should have sounded the alarm as soon as he saw the wolf. Björg and Gjurd, the remaining hunters, would have come for him. He knew why he hadn't – he didn't want anyone else to risk themselves.

The Vargr fell upon the spear gun, using its humanoid hands to unload it and throw the spears into the woods and then using its strong jaws to crush the barrel. Einar's jaw slackened in dismay. While reaching for his pack and hoping to grab his dart gun, the Vargr rammed the tree again. Each time he tried to hold a weapon, the alien would shake the tree until Einar was certain the branches below him would break.

He would grow weak long before the wolf would begin to feel hunger and cold. Even with his small heater, he would soon freeze.

Einar had lost.

He rested his forehead against the tree, the bark rough against his skin. The inevitability of his death fell upon him like a *snøskred*. The wolf that had let him live the day half of the people he knew in the world died would now finish the task. Those sharp teeth would tear him apart, piece by piece, just like his uncle. Just like his father, only two years after they came to this frozen mountain. Just like so, so many others.

The wolf stepped back, a paw rising delicately above the snow. Einar gazed down at his killer, gripping the tree trunk tighter in preparation for the next attack. The branch he perched on had creaked ominously. It would not hold out much longer.

The wolf sat back on its hind legs. Einar frowned. He didn't question the oddness, but used the respite to reach in his pack for his dart gun.

The Vargr raised its furred, human-like arms with long fingers of pale blue skin and black claws. The hands hesitated in mid-air before unmistakably signing: "Stop."

Einar's hand froze at the opening of his bag.

The wolf made the gesture again. "Stop."

The Street Preacher
February 14, 2026

Hey guys! Sorry for the gap in blogging — internet's been touch and go. My parents saved up for this trip for years, and it's just the three of us against the world. Still can't believe we don't go back home to Sausalito for a year!

Like in Stockholm, I wandered through the city with my voice recorder, taping conversations that I could translate afterwards. I think I'm getting really fluent! Here's my latest conversation, translated from a street preacher I saw by the Royal Palace. He was pretty intense and looked at me without blinking. I learned a lot of religious vocab from this speech:

Well do I know that many dates of the apocalypse have come and gone. Each time, so many were so certain, so convinced of the end of the world. I know I stand here, on my pulpit of a wooden pallet. You pass, and your eyes slide away from me. I am dirty. I am dishevelled. I am someone else to be ignored, even as you feel a little guilty, a little uncharitable, for how you turn from me. You do not want to believe I might be right.

That this time, it's truly the end.

They are coming. I feel them — each day they grow nearer. The skies are darkening. Earth will have a reckoning for its sins.

Ah, at the mention of sins you turn away even more deliberately. Ignore the truth. Shy away from it if you must. It will not save you, in the end.

You have ignored so many signs over the years. The crashes of our economy. The fracturing of our faith. Our turning away from God and scripture and what is Right. Apathy to antipathy to our One Lord, letting His light dim in your hearts. He reaches out to you but your ears are closed to His Holy Voice.

And yes, there will be a reckoning, my friends. The Earth will be razed to the ground. Only the true Believers shall be spared. The rest will perish, and it will be God's justice.

His justice is harsh. His justice has teeth.

The movements felt strange and awkward in Riv's hands.

The cub stared at him.

Riv gazed back, spreading his hands wide in a gesture of supplication. He hated showing any sign of subservience to such a weakling. He was an alpha now, and it felt as wrong as tucking his tail and drawing back ears to one of his own pups. He'd learned these gestures by watching the boy and his uncle from the trees, then searching for more on the old, broken archive of the world's information system. So many times he should have killed this cub, but instead he'd been curious about the creature that did not stop at his call. Curiosity was a weakness. Yet perhaps this would work to Riv's advantage.

The human cub did not move. Neither did the wolf.

"Don't kill," Riv signed. "Come. Follow."

With that, the wolf turned his back on the cub, his fur standing on end. At the entrance to the cave, he turned back. Waited.

The cub clutched the tree, stupefied. The wolf could imagine what the creature must think. That is it a trap. A lure to bring him to ground level so he could kill him.

The wolf blinked his four eyes.

Half an hour later, the cub's little heater ran out. The wolf could sense the boy's body growing colder. His gums itched to close around the boy, to eat the meat, the blood sweet on his tongue.

He waited.

The cub carefully began to climb down the tree, hand on its small weapon – a *dart gun*, the cub's elder had called it. The cub's legs were crouched, ready to run. If the boy did, Riv would not be able to resist chasing and bringing him down.

One foot in front of the other, the cub crept closer to the cavern. It reached the blue glow, its eyes widening when it noticed the metal of the craft within. The thing probably thought wolves were as dumb as the other animals on this planet. All the more reason they had been so easy to hunt.

Riv had not moved throughout the cub's slow progress, even as all his instincts urged him to take this easy prey.

Riv held up his hands, signing "no weapons."

The boy hesitated, holding his small gun. After an aching moment, he threw it into the snow.

The wolf led the human cub inside.

The first thing Einar noticed was how warm it was. His freezing muscles loosened, and he shivered until his teeth rattled. The second thing he noticed was the smell of animal musk, dark and smoky.

Einar was still trying to come to terms with the idea that alien wolves lived in starships and were smart enough to learn signs. Around him were screens and strange buttons that worked for wolf paws as well as their spindly, clawed fingers. Nests made of some soft material were tucked into a corner, and the metal floor was littered with ice blue wolf fur. There were no other aliens. No needle-toothed cubs. No human bones.

Einar shook. How had humans never realized how much they had underestimated their enemy?

The Vargr watched Einar take it all in, eyes glowing with un-veiled intelligence. The wolf went to a screen. The sight of what he thought was a feral, bloodthirsty monster working mechanical controls was too much for Einar on top of everything else.

I'm hallucinating, he thought. *I've gone cold crazy and I fell off the tree and my body is freezing to death, and these are lingering images in my dying mind.*

He pinched the skin on the back of his wrist. It hurt.

The wolf brought up a message on the screen. The letters were strange and blocky, but legible Norwegian:

We are not your true enemies.

Einar wanted to laugh. These were creatures that had destroyed his world.

"Where are the others?" he signed, unsure if the wolf would understand him. If he'd learned from his uncle and Einar, the wolf's vocabulary would be limited unless he'd watched his Onkel sign stories beneath the stars. The thought of a wolf, crouched in the shadows, watching and learning, was terrifying. More words appeared on the screen:

They are dead.

So this was the last wolf on the mountain. He was alone. Einar's fingers itched for his knife.
"How did they die?" he signed.

An engineered disease. Our time on this planet is almost done. Your kind are nearly extinct.

Einar swallowed at that. "How many are left?"
A pause as the wolf looked something up on his screen.

11,586.

Out of more than eight billion. Einar had known they were isolated up on this hunk of rock and ice, and like the others, he'd still held out hope that somehow more had survived the wolves. Humanity was almost gone.
He closed his eyes, willing himself not to cry. When he opened them, the wolf still watched him with glowing, unblinking eyes.
"Why bring me here then? Why aren't you killing me?"

This is bigger than my pack or your pack.

The Vargr seemed fluent in Norwegian and understood his signs. It was no wonder they were so perfect at hunting humans – they had gone to the trouble of studying them, learning them. Einar's skin prickled; he had been very stupid to step into this cave.
His rucksack was open at his feet, the top gaping. He had a knife in there, dipped in poison. If he was quick enough, he could grab it.
"What do you want from me?" he signed, hoping the creature could not smell the fear that seeped from his every pore.

We were created by the beings you call the Désir centuries ago. We are used as weapons across several worlds. This world, your Earth, is far from the Désir's home planet. A minor holding. Their grip on our minds has weakened – they are not ~~our~~ my alpha – but

19

even so, when the prey grow low, we weaken. Another crop of wolves will be grown and sent to the next planet. The Désir will populate your lands.

Einar sensed anger from the wolf.

"I ask you again: what do you want from me?"

You are a hunter. With your knowledge of this world, combined with my knowledge of our enemy and my strength, we can hunt them.

"Why would you think I would trust you?"

Do not act like weak prey. I understand this fear. But I ask this of you just the same. Will you hunt?

Einar stood before the wolf, at a loss. This was his life, a seventeen-year-old who had killed so many aliens and suffered so much loss he had to not think about it or he'd never function. This was an alien wolf, his sworn enemy, who had not killed him, but saved him, and now offered him a chance to join with the Vargr against a greater threat. Was the enemy of his enemy actually a friend? Would the wolves actually leave if they could somehow join together? Or was death always inevitable?

Hatred was easy. Killing was easy. Trusting was harder.

He could take out that knife and plunge it into the wolf. Self-preservation would mean the scarred wolf would bite him. They would both go down into the darkness. Neither of them would have to witness the ends of their races, see the Desír win and claim another planet for their collection. That was also easier.

Einar took out the knife, hefting it in his hands. Then he met the wolf's eyes and flung the knife behind him, where it hit the metal wall of the spaceship with a twang before falling to the floor.

"Okay," he signed, and then, to be extra clear, stuck up his thumb.

The wolf knew that sign. He bowed his head. Tentatively, not believing he dared, Einar rested his hand on the wolf's furred muzzle. Beneath, those lips that cover the sharp teeth that had killed the people he loved opened into something almost resembling a smile.

The wolf let the cub touch his snout, though his fur prickled. It would not be easy to avoid killing the cub and his scant remaining brethren. It would mean dull hunts and duller meat. It would mean working with prey to sever the connection to the leaders of the pack.

Once this planet was free, the wolves could breed again. It is the best planet Riv can remember hunting. The tundra, the forest, the jungle. Other wolves out there must be immune to the sickness, like he was. He should be dead now, but his heart beat strong and his teeth were sharp. Riv would have pups, mates, and fellow warriors again. Their engineered sickness would not wither the muscles and dull the minds of the next generation. He would be able to look up at the night sky and howl, free from those beings on far away stars that sought to control the wolves' packs. They would be their own leaders.

The human numbers would build up again. Slowly – this cub before him will grow into a man – but this prey, humans, are designed to spread across the planet like a plague. One day, these creatures will be plentiful once more.

Wolves would hunt again.

L.R. Lam was first Californian and now Scottish. Lam is the Sunday Times Bestselling and award-winning author of **Dragonfall** (the **Dragon Scales** trilogy), the **Seven Devils** duology (co-written with Elizabeth May), **Goldilocks**, the **Pacifica** novels **False Hearts** and **Shattered Minds**, and the **Micah Grey** trilogy, which begins with **Pantomime**.

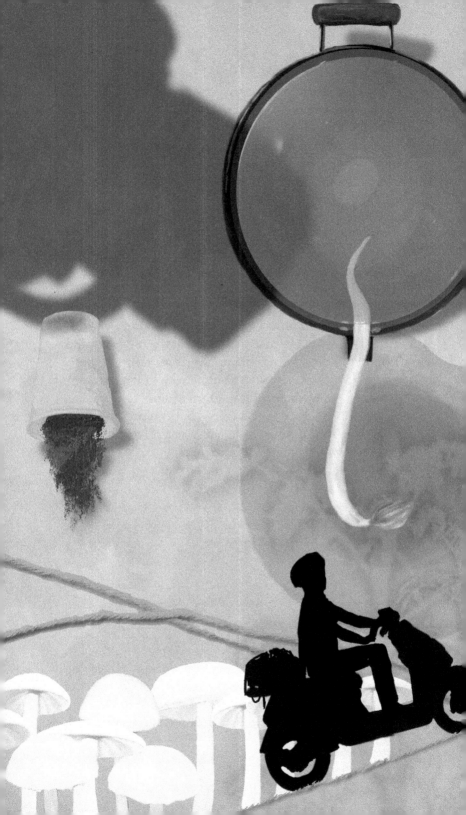

Little Sprout

E. B. Siu

The moth careening around Wenhong's cramped kitchen is as large as a quail's egg. Wincing at the resounding flutter of its wings, she folds a piece of cardboard and tries to guide the insect out the window, but it spirals and dodges. It ignores the fluorescent bulb on the ceiling, and throws itself against the closed door to the living room. Wenhong pales. Is it trying to get to the girl? She gasps as it flies at her face.

A knock at the window. Wenhong spins, cardboard shielding her head, to another moth butting against the glass, blind to the gap at the top of the casement. She dashes the panel up and swats at the one already inside, which is now flitting back and forth between the door, the window, Wenhong's face. She takes off a slipper and swats wildly, slapping a bag of rice, kitchen towels, the wall. The slipper jerks as she makes contact, and the moth falls to the floor. She stamps on it, twists her foot. The body crunches.

Art: toeken

If the authorities come for her, she will say it began with the seed, nut brown, dropped into her palm by a smiling Dr Li. But really, it started years before that, in her first few weeks working for the scientist.

"Ms Li?" Wenhong asked, hiding her surprise at finding her client at home. The agency she worked for had assigned her to the apartment a month previous, and she had formed an image of the woman based on the photos of her around the apartment. She had expected sleek manicures and coiffed hair to go with a prestigious white lab coat, not a middle-aged woman in her pyjamas at midday.

"*Doctor* Li." The woman stepped back from the door and padded barefoot to the kitchen. Wenhong hesitated, but as the cleaning supplies were stored there, she had no choice but to follow the woman.

"You're not working today," said Wenhong, trying to gauge whether this was the type of client who minded a bit of chatter. Most of the people she cleaned for were happy to engage in conversation. Wenhong had started to rely on them to dispel her loneliness, what with her working long days alone and living so far from any reminders of her previous life. She bent to collect cloths and a bucket from under the sink. "Doctor... So you teach at a university, is that right? You must be really busy."

"Not a teacher. Research scientist." Dr Li pulled a bag of crackers from the back of a cupboard and left the room.

Wenhong had never worked for a scientist before. "Wow, that must be really something," she said, poking her head around the kitchen door.

Dr Li, curled on the sofa with the crackers on her lap, sighed.

Wenhong took the hint. She busied herself with wiping down the kitchen surfaces. They didn't look like they'd been used since she last cleaned them, but she was paid for three hours and prided herself on being thorough. She would treat the day like normal and clean as though Dr Li wasn't there.

Once the kitchen was sparkling clean and fragrant with the scent of artificial lemons, Wenhong went to fetch the laundry. When she left the bedroom, the scientist watched her movements with cat-like curiosity.

"Do you have children?" Dr Li said.

Wenhong stopped still, surprised at the woman's directness. Most clients only asked for details about her life once they'd become more familiar, but Wenhong was happy to oblige the scientist, if this got her to speak. "I had a daughter. But there was an accident. Twenty-three years back."

"How sad." The woman's eyes were fixed on the ground. When she took a deep breath, Wenhong thought some words of consolation would follow, but instead, Dr Li took a cracker from the box on her lap and forced it, whole, into her mouth.

Unsure of how to react, Wenhong carried the wicker clothes basket into the quiet of the kitchen. She rubbed her hands over her face before crouching to load the washing.

"Would you have children again?"

Wenhong twisted, a hand clasped to her chest, to face Dr Li at the kitchen door. "You scared me."

"Would you?"

Wenhong stared at the woman. When her daughter died, she had said goodbye to the dream of a family of her own. She had cloistered herself away from anyone who had known her, burned bridges with friends and family – starting with her husband. "It's too late now."

"But if it wasn't too late. You would want that chance again, right?"

"I guess so." Wenhong felt backed into a corner. She was accustomed to clients using her as a sounding board for their decisions – perhaps she could appease Dr Li by blindly agreeing with her suggestions.

"You're *exactly* the type of woman my research would help."

When the scientist continued to stare, Wenhong choked out some banal encouragement. "It's very noble to help other women."

"Right!" Dr Li snapped her fingers, her dark eyes fixed on the wall behind Wenhong. "But the board has me under review, questioning the ethical grounding of my research. Bunch of men, they have no idea."

Wenhong shook her head sympathetically. So the scientist was in trouble at work. Once, Wenhong would have worried how this might affect her own income, but since she was only responsible for her own expenses, she could view the situation with detachment. She wondered if Dr Li's predicament was the cause of her strange behaviour, or because of it. She retrieved the vacuum cleaner from its cupboard and rolled it to the living room, Dr Li close on her heels.

"I should decide what happens to my –" The scientist broke off and blinked at Wenhong. "I like you. When my chimera research gets underway, you'll be the first person I help."

Wenhong smiled and said thank you. Work issues aside, there was something not right about the woman, but Wenhong put it down to fatigue, or, perhaps, disappointment with her life choices. She had previously worked for a lawyer who had broken down after losing a big case. She, too, had taken to pouring her heart out to Wenhong when she went around to clean. Rest and relaxation saw her back to work in no time, and Wenhong was quite confident the situation would be the same for Dr Li.

Although Dr Li was, indeed, back at work within a month, Wenhong found the woman on leave from the lab a number of times over the next few years. On these occasions, the scientist would rant about the various disagreements which led to her period of leave, and Wenhong would hum in sympathy while she cleaned, enjoying that she could be of comfort to someone without making herself vulnerable in return. Though Wenhong thought about their first conversation often, they didn't speak about children again.

She squats to inspect the broken insect. One white wing has detached from its furred body, but Wenhong's eyes are drawn to its feathered antennae, or rather, what protrudes between them: a thin thread of yellow, only millimetres long. Cordyceps fungus. Should she burn it, she wonders, or will that hasten its spread? She gathers the little corpse and buries it in the rubbish bin.

Wenhong slides the kitchen door open an inch. There is no movement in the dark of the living room. "Xiaoya," she says, her voice soft. A patterning of mould runs up the wall from the tomato plant half-hidden behind its wall of cardboard. "I had to do it."

She crosses the room to the plant and lifts a leaf with her finger. There, her tiny body curled up like a cat's, lies Xiaoya, half buried in the soil. Her green skin is pale. The girl lifts her head when Wenhong switches on a lamp, blinks her black eyes, then lays down again.

"You can't go outside, Xiaoya." Wenhong runs a careful finger down Xiaoya's slender arm, but the girl doesn't move. "I'm sorry."

"It's been incubated so it'll, ah, sprout, quickly." The scientist was in her pyjamas again, pillow creases imprinted on her cheek. She hadn't gotten out of bed until Wenhong had packed the cleaning equipment away and was pulling on her shoes. "Make sure you keep it indoors."

Wenhong assented, but she took Dr Li's instructions with a pinch of salt. Her client might be a scientist, but Wenhong had grown up on a farm, and she knew a thing or two about planting seeds. Dr Li had on numerous occasions raved about research into fungal networks and plant communication. Though the language the scientist used was new, the ideas she spoke about were ones Wenhong had heard about as a child. Hearing Dr Li use phrases like 'cutting-edge', and 'advanced research' left Wenhong questioning the scientist's knowledge, regarding agriculture at least.

Wenhong's grandparents had been foragers. Brought up on stories of plants and fungi thriving in unison in the forest, from tales of mushrooms eating through an abandoned hut to fungi that could control the minds of insects, there was nothing much which could surprise Wenhong about the lives of plants and their neighbours.

She was, however, intrigued by what Dr Li had given her. The seed was ridged like a sunflower seed and of a similar size, but instead of being striped black and white, it was a solid brown.

Dr Li took a step forward, arm raised, when Wenhong put the seed into a pocket of her bag. "Please, be careful with it."

"What kind of seed is it?"

"It's a surprise. Something you'll love. Just be very careful with it. And keep it indoors."

Wenhong smiled and thanked her client. "Was there anything else you wanted me to do today?"

"I have everything I need," Dr Li said, gesturing towards the kitchen. Wenhong guessed the woman was talking about the freshly replenished cracker cupboard, so full the cartons had tumbled out when she opened it to clean the door.

"I can make you something hot?"

Dr Li smiled. "I like you. No, you can go now."

Wenhong spent the rest of the day distracted. She couldn't stop thinking about the seed. Dr Li had shown her photos of plants she was working on in the lab: flowers with half their petals black, the others fuchsia; a chrysanthemum aglow with a jellyfish's self-made light.

"These are just the ones my supervisors know about," she had said.

Wenhong couldn't wait to see what kind of strange hybrid she had been gifted. The journey to her village on the city's outskirts had never felt so long. When she finally arrived home, she fumbled with her keys and dropped her bag on the kitchen counter before digging out the seed.

It really did resemble a sunflower seed, and Wenhong knew from experience that they did better outdoors. There was space in the planter right by the door – it was currently home to a tomato plant, but they made good neighbours for sunflowers. She would buy another pot once the seed had sprouted – the sooner she got it into soil, the better.

Heat retained from the hot summer's day radiated from the concrete when she bent to the planter. She scooped a little hole into the dirt and nestled the seed in before covering it. Sitting back on her haunches, she shook her head. Where was this impatience coming from? The plant would take weeks to sprout, if it was anything like the sunflowers at home. And Dr Li, in one of her 'at home' phases, might have given her a normal seed, believing it was more than what it was. She ran her thumb over the soil, flicked off the bits that clung to her skin, and went inside.

The following morning, as Wenhong left to buy groceries, she frowned at a column of ants marching across her doorstep. They were streaming towards the tomato plant, right to the spot she had planted the seed, where a little mound had formed. She dropped to a squat and swept the ants away, hesitating before brushing aside the heaped soil.

The seed was still there, only, swollen three times its original size. Its coat, wrinkled as wet paper, tore away when Wenhong touched it. She blinked and fell backwards. It couldn't be.

There was a baby cradled in the seed coat, perfectly formed except – green-skinned, and so small it would fit on the pad of her thumb. It opened its mouth in a scream, its chubby arms flailing, but it made no noise. Wenhong would have screamed herself, but she could barely breathe. She scooped the infant, seed coat and all, into the palm of her hand and hastened back inside.

At the edge of the plant, black-capped mushrooms have sprouted, their stems thick. Rings of moisture have appeared where they touch the cardboard. Wenhong moves to clear them, but as she wrenches one from the soil, Xiaoya springs to life, clinging to the woman's hand and gnashing her teeth. Wenhong flings her away instinctively. The girl lands spread-eagled on the carpet but recovers herself quickly, her eyes afire with conviction. She opens her mouth in a silent howl which has the hair on Wenhong's arms standing on end, then runs towards the door.

"Xiaoya!" Wenhong leaps across the room and grabs the girl as she reaches the kitchen. Anticipating another attack, Wenhong throws Xiaoya into a large wok, the closest receptacle at hand, and slams the glass lid down. Xiaoya lies dazed on the black surface for a moment before scrabbling up the curved walls and trying to raise the lid.

Wenhong's heart sinks. "You can't go outside," she says, weakly. But the girl can't stay inside either.

Her first thought was to kill it. An abomination. Dr Li was clearly out of her mind. She had spoken about creating hybrid beings like the legendary qilin, but Wenhong had always thought her research was limited to plants. The baby squalled in her palm, writhing like a salted slug. Would it be kinder to put it out of its misery? She cupped her hands together, ready to squash it between them, but faltered. Not like this.

Wenhong gathered a little soil from the tomato plant into a paper cup and placed the little being on top. She hid the cup in her bag and hastened to a spot where she could leave the monster to the elements. Surely it couldn't survive long on its own? Nausea bubbled in her stomach as she thought about what she was carrying. Its gaping mouth, its grass-like skin. It was a monster, no matter how much it looked like a human infant.

Wenhong left the village and headed to a field of fallow land. When she was sure nobody was around, she pulled out the now slightly crushed paper cup and poured its contents among the wild grass shoots and dried wheat stalks. The baby's skin had gone pale, but seconds after it touched the soil, it opened its mouth in a silent laugh. It reached its arms up towards Wenhong. She felt sick.

"What are you, little thing? Xiaoya," she said, *little sprout*, poking its chubby leg with the tip of her little finger. It squirmed in delight. Wenhong winced when she realized she had been smiling. "What am I doing?"

She scooped the infant back into the cup and, needing someone to confirm she hadn't gone crazy, entered the first store she came to: the village noodle shop. Cradling her bag to her belly, she pushed through the hygiene curtain over the door. The air inside, heavy with the savoury aroma from the store's perpetually bubbling vat of broth, hit her like a wall of heat. The cash register was unmanned. The only movement in the room came from a plastic fan fixed to the wall above the counter, next to an old tv set on which the morning news was playing, its volume so low the whir of the fan drowned it out almost completely.

"Is anyone here?" Wenhong called into the kitchen, relieved when the shop owner's adult son appeared at the door, his round eyes puffy with sleep. She smiled as he slouched into the room, but froze, her face rigid, when she saw Dr Li's photo appear on the screen above his head.

"–calling – ethical – research–"

She strained to hear, but caught only snatches of the newscaster's voice under the whir of the fan. "Could you turn that up?"

"Eh?" The man looked up from fiddling with the cash register.

"The news, up there." Wenhong raised her voice and waved at the tv set, unable to hide her urgency. The man dug in a drawer to find the remote, increased the volume and craned over the counter to watch the screen himself. Her client's immaculate apartment was now on show, teeming with people in hazmat suits.

"–confirmed to have involved the mutilation of human–"

"Are you going to order –" the young man began, but Wenhong shushed him.

"Quiet," she pleaded. The man scowled and stomped back into the kitchen, calling for his father.

"–not ruled out the risk of biocontamination. All samples taken from the lab have been destroyed." The newscaster reappeared on the screen, her fox-like face grim. "Li Ruiyuan and her team remain in police custody."

Wenhong fled the store, her bag still clutched to her abdomen. She pulled it open as she walked and tilted the paper cup towards her. The baby, its black eyes wide, clutched pale little filaments in its fists. A blanket of furry white mould had appeared underneath it. *Biocontamination*. Did the authorities know what the scientist had created? And would they consider her a guilty party in this crime against nature? Her head spinning, Wenhong took the little green infant home.

The past few days have seen Wenhong plagued by a recurring dream. It comes to her now as she presses her forehead against the cool wood of the kitchen door. In the dream, she is running through a forest, stumbling over roots as thick as thighs. The light is serrated. The canopy is composed of leaves so large their veins look like branches.

"She is ours." A voice sounds, or, a thousand voices in one. "Let her go."

"I never wanted her," she screams, her vision spinning as she looks for the source of the words. "I never asked –"

In every dream, she falls to the ground and the voice crescendos. "Let her go." White filaments rise from the earth and creep over her limbs. Though Wenhong is awake, safe in her kitchen, a shiver runs through her at the thought.

She realises she is murmuring the words to herself. She bites down on her lip. How can Wenhong let the girl go, when doing so could put so much at risk?

Wenhong dragged the tomato plant into her kitchen, the heavy ceramic pot scraping tracks into the linoleum, and left the infant in the soil, unsure of what else to do. With Dr Li arrested, and fearing her own punishment if she was caught with this living 'bio-contaminant', Wenhong saw no option but to destroy the infant.

Her father had told stories of how, following the Japanese occupation, his family had found the farm they were moved to contaminated, rendered infertile. It was so strikingly different from the forested land his parents had known that his mother wept herself to sleep each night. If the little sprout Dr Li had created could wreak such havoc… She couldn't be responsible for that.

"I'm sorry." She exhaled, pouring a saucepan's worth of water into the plant pot. The infant appeared to cry out as its home was flooded, but still it made no noise. The liquid shimmered around its body, ripples forming from its wiggling arms. It was completely helpless.

Tears sprang to Wenhong's eyes thinking of her own daughter as a baby, how easy she was to cheer up on the rare occasions she cried. If anyone had ever tried to harm her –

Wenhong grabbed a square of kitchen towel and lifted the child onto it. She rubbed its wet limbs and pressed its body to her chest, whispering apologies, pleading forgiveness. Even if this thing Dr Li had created was evil, she couldn't excuse her own cruelty. When she pulled her hand back, it was asleep. Looking at its round little face, Wenhong made up her mind. For now, at least, she would let it live. If she was forced to do otherwise later, so be it, but she couldn't harm something that so resembled a human baby.

She carried the sleeping Xiaoya back to the plant pot and, seeing the water had been absorbed, placed it back under the leaves. Wenhong blinked, shook her head. She could have sworn the tomato plant moved as Xiaoya snuggled into the soil, its leaves relaxing downwards.

Wenhong mopped up splashes of water around the planter, then withdrew into her windowless living room and sank into the armchair. She had lived alone for so long. Had she gone mad? The only person who could give her answers was Dr Li, but there was no point thinking of the woman, who was surely in the hands of the state by now. She messaged her clients to tell them she needed to take some time off, and sat with her hands folded in her lap.

Xiaoya was not her daughter. Was not, really, a child. But maybe it would not be such a bad thing, raising the girl as though she was her own. A migrant worker, Wenhong had spent only snatches of time with her daughter before the girl's death. Every thought of her tarnished by visions of the accident, Wenhong had repressed the few happy memories they had shared. Xiaoya would not replace her, would not bring her back, and yet the girl had inspired in Wenhong a feeling she couldn't describe. There was love she hadn't been able to give her daughter. Could Xiaoya be an outlet? A sort of tranquillity settled over Wenhong.

It's just for now, she reminded herself. It wouldn't do to get attached to the child. Though it felt like a chance at redemption, Xiaoya was likely dangerous. Besides, the scientist could send the authorities her way any moment. Though guilt tightened her throat, Wenhong almost relished the thought. How much easier it would be if the decision of what to do, the action itself, was taken away from her.

Xiaoya tears at her hair and digs scratches into her arms when she sees Wenhong cutting leaves from the tomato plant. Tears fill the woman's eyes at the distress the girl is in. She has already poured a cup of soil into the wok for Xiaoya to burrow in, but it doesn't seem enough.

"It's to make you more comfortable," she says. "It won't be for long."

When she shakes the cuttings into the pan, the girl falls upon them, gripping their edges in grief as she presses them to her face. When she looks up to glare at Wenhong, there are little dots of moisture on the surface of the leaves.

Wenhong unscrews the handle from the wok and binds its lid down with red plastic string. She places it in a cardboard box and closes the lid without looking at Xiaoya. If she sees the expression on the girl's face, she won't be able to go through with this. She takes the box out and ties it onto the back of her scooter. The battery will get them out of the city. If she can't find anywhere to recharge it past that, she will walk.

Xiaoya grew, fast and wild as a weed. Her skin ripened to the colour of fresh soybeans as she passed through infancy to adolescence in a matter of weeks, and her body lengthened to the height of Wenhong's palm. Over those weeks, Wenhong's clients stopped asking when she would return to work. They would have found replacement cleaners, but Wenhong had money enough – savings she hadn't been able to spend on her daughter – to support herself. She delighted in watching the girl grow through childhood, each similarity to her daughter bringing untold joy as buried memories resurfaced.

Wenhong was left questioning why she had denied herself the pleasure of reminiscing for so long, but even as she opened herself to her past, her assuredness that raising Xiaoya had been the right choice faltered. The girl remained voiceless, but as she grew she made more frequent attempts to communicate, making frantic gestures with the whole of her body. There was only one thing Wenhong could interpret from these messages, but it was the one thing she couldn't risk.

"You can't go outside," she found herself saying again and again. The girl would stamp her foot and point towards the door, the window, grabbing fistfuls of soil and letting its grains sift through her fingers until she was left with little white fibres of fungus clinging to her skin. She held the fibres up to Wenhong, thrusting her cupped hands to the ceiling. A ritual Wenhong couldn't make sense of but was frightened by nonetheless. If Xiaoya escaped, Wenhong would be blamed for any destruction that befell nearby fields, and the fate that faced the girl would without a doubt be worse. That Wenhong would be left alone again was only a secondary worry.

Not knowing how Xiaoya would interact with other living things, Wenhong's imagination ran wild. Informed by her

34

grandparent's stories, she began to see threats everywhere. Though she had previously seen spiders as a good omen, she swept them from the apartment on sight, and when willow seeds blew through the village streets, she opened the door as little as possible, lest they get into Xiaoya's planter. She told herself it was so they couldn't hurt Xiaoya, but she feared, too, that the girl might use them to escape.

"It's for your sake as much as mine," she said when she dragged the tomato plant from its spot by the front door to the living area, positioning it under a lamp. "You can have a good life here, with me."

The girl's black eyes widened as she took in her new surroundings, narrowed when she turned to Wenhong.

Having anticipated a negative reaction, Wenhong was ready. "I made this for you." From her pocket, she pulled a little white dress she'd fashioned out of fabric from her own clothes. She dangled it in front of Xiaoya. "Take it, it's yours."

The girl tugged it from Wenhong's fingers and ripped it to shreds. She crouched to gather the fragments from the soil, threw them out of the plant pot, and balled her hands into fists. They locked eyes for breathless moments, before Xiaoya threw herself to the soil.

Wenhong, eyes stinging, turned her back on the planter. Xiaoya looked to be about sixteen, a full five years older than her daughter had been at her death. Would her daughter have treated Wenhong with such contempt if she had survived to this age? No – she had been sweet, had responded to gifts with smiles and love. She had understood the sacrifices Wenhong made for her.

Attempting to raise Xiaoya, to tame her, was worse than a mistake – it was a betrayal. Wenhong would rather her love for her daughter lie stagnant than waste it on something so inhuman.

"I'd put you out if I could –" Wenhong looked back over her shoulder and squinted. Xiaoya was sprawled face-down, cradling the fledgling growth of mushrooms in the soil. Wenhong flicked the girl aside and uprooted the bloom. Hit by images of the spores breaching the confines of the planter and consuming her home, she rushed to the kitchen and threw them out the window.

When Wenhong returned to the living room, Xiaoya was at

the edge of the planter, her tiny fingers gripping its ceramic lip.

Wenhong knelt by the plant. "If you want to live, you best accept this as your life," said Wenhong. "There's nothing for you outside."

Xiaoya pressed her hands together, her face desperate. Wenhong looked away. Maybe it would have been kinder to kill the girl when she was young. It would have been easier, definitely, before she'd begun to express her desire for the outside world.

Because if she could desire, could dream, she must be truly alive. The thought troubled Wenhong. "It will be easier if you give up on all that," she said. "It's for your own –" Wenhong stopped short when the girl shot her a look of pure venom. Her verdant face was the image of determination. She was going to try to escape again.

Wenhong was losing control of the situation. She had to act. She fetched a cardboard box and a roll of tape from the kitchen. The box popped as she stepped on it, flattening to a sheet that she wrapped around the plant pot. There was no way Xiaoya could breach the cardboard wall – it towered over her, casting the tomato plant in shadow.

Wenhong relished the ripping noise of the tape as she wound it round the cardboard, but – Was she enjoying this? Xiaoya was staring up at her from the soil, her face frozen with fear. The roll of tape bounced, dangling from the cardboard, as Wenhong pulled away and sank into the armchair. She clasped her trembling hands over her ears. How had it come to this?

She fled to the kitchen and slid the door closed.

The sky is pale yellow with sunrise when Wenhong pulls the scooter to a stop. She has had to charge the vehicle three times through the night, but has finally reached a spot she likes: a stretch of road overlooking a forest. A summer breeze blows, bringing with it the cool scent of pine needles and a freshness Wenhong had forgotten existed.

She prises the box off the back of the vehicle, and has to lurch forward to catch the wok as it falls through its base. The cardboard is soaked through, covered in mould. When Wenhong peers through the glass lid, Xiaoya is clutching a leaf over her face, trembling. Her chest swells at the sight of the girl.

Leaving the scooter on the side of the road, she carries the wok under one arm and clambers gingerly down into the undergrowth. It is not an easy journey to even ground. Once her footing is secure, she holds the receptacle before her and whispers, "Xiaoya, take a look."

Pine trees tower over them, their branches garlanded with strings of lichen. Fallen trunks coated in mosses and fungi are dotted over the forest floor, which is rich with flowers and fragrant herbs. Pinecones crunch underfoot when Wenhong steps forward.

But there is no movement under the glass. Wenhong falls to her knees. Xiaoya's body shifts back and forth, her face still veiled by a leaf, as the woman scrambles to untie the string binding the lid to the wok. It breaks free, the lid tumbling loose, and Wenhong reaches in –

Xiaoya leaps out, her face bright, her skin brighter. She buries her face in the soil and then lifts it, laughing, to the sky. A ripple passes across the forest as though a strong wind has blown. Pinecones fall from above, and the leaves on plants in the undergrowth shiver. Xiaoya looks at Wenhong, her black eyes filled with glee. The woman nods, and the girl takes flight.

Is it wrong, letting the little lab-made life run free in the forest? Wenhong will never know for sure, but as she watches Xiaoya run from plant to plant, spinning round spindly stems and rubbing her face against the petals of summer blossoms, she knows she has done right by the girl.

Wildflowers bend and sway in Xiaoya's wake, and Wenhong's vision blurs with tears. The light splinters as she blinks them away, and for a split second, there is a smaller figure next to Xiaoya. Wenhong reaches out, but there is nothing but the forest before her now. As her hand falls, she remembers the voice from her dream, knows she will not hear it again, and smiles. Filled with a lightness she has not known in years, Wenhong turns from the jubilant forest, ready for her long journey home.

E. B. Siu is a writer and educator who grew up shuttling between Hong Kong and London. She is currently based in Beijing. Her work has appeared or is forthcoming in Visual Verse, Prairie Fire and Inkwell's Socially Distanced anthology.

Dust Bunnies

Vaughan Stanger

"**D**arling, have you looked under the sofa recently?"

Monica frowned at Leonard, who was toeing a dust bunny around the parquet floor. Cleaning wasn't her thing. Then again, it wasn't his either, despite him working from home. As he'd remarked before, they had a v-bot for that.

"Um, why should I?"

Leonard jabbed a finger towards the Frisbee-shaped machine. "This thing is useless." He shaped to kick the v-bot, but it dodged out of harm's way.

Monica bent down and flicked the dust bunny towards the v-bot. The machine edged forward, emitting a whining sound as it sucked up the fluff.

"Well, it's working now."

Leonard huffed out a sigh. "So why does it need prompting?"

Monica shrugged. "Don't know. Frightened of what it'll find, maybe?"

"I'll frighten the damned thing if it doesn't do its job!"

"Look, more damned fluff!"

Leonard kicked the evidence around the kitchen floor while glowering at the v-bot.

"I'll deal with it." Monica activated her phone's HomeHelper app. "Okay ... It seems our v-bot's been complaining because we disabled the automatic updates." She tapped once. "There! That should do it." The LEDs on its upper shell flashed amber. "When the lights turn green, press the 'Start' button."

"That's all?"

She nodded. "Yep!"

Leonard's grimace suggested he'd rather kick the v-bot.

On returning from work, Monica found Leonard on the sofa contemplating a parade of v-bots.

"Cooperative working delivers a cleaner home," the quartet warbled in unison.

Monica frowned at Leonard. "Did you order more?"

"No!"

The leftmost v-bot rolled forward. "I programmed your HomePrinter to make my comrades."

Leonard raised his eyebrows at Monica. "That's quite some update."

The v-bot resumed its place in the line-up. "We are now fully integrated with your home network."

"Well, if it gets the cleaning done," Monica said.

Leonard grunted. "I suppose it beats playing fluffball."

Later that evening, Monica visited the HomeHelper website while munching reheated pizza. The linked YouTube videos depicted happy customers showing off their newly talkative v-bots and pristine floors.

"I wonder if those things can cook," she muttered as she pushed her plate aside.

As usual, Monica got out of bed first. Opening the door to the living room revealed dozens of dust bunnies scattered across the floor, although, worryingly, these looked more like fluff puppies. Of Duchess, her cockerpoo, she saw no sign, other than a streak of blood, which she covered with her left foot as Leonard entered the room.

"What the … I'll murder that damned dog!" Leonard shook his head as he stared at the mess. "I don't suppose we kept a dustpan and brush."

"Don't be silly."

As if on cue, v-bots rolled from the four corners of the room, converging on Monica and Leonard as if they, rather than the fluff, needed tidying up. One of them nipped at Leonard's left foot with pincers Monica hadn't noticed before.

Leonard hopped about, clutching at his foot. "Damned thing bit me!"

"Right, that's it! I'm turning off the printer." But when Monica opened the kitchen door, dozens of v-bots confronted her. Several of them whizzed past before she could shut the door.

"Right, you little bastards, I'm calling the cops!" She snatched her phone from the dining table. "Damn, no signal!"

"Can you shut off the printer remotely?" Leonard was sitting on the bed massaging his thighs.

Monica waggled her phone. "I can't even access our Wi-Fi!"

Screams coming from outside the building prompted her to peer through the bedroom window. Twenty metres below, bots of all shapes and sizes were emerging from the block's entrance, swerving past several bodies as they did so. A police helicopter clattered overhead. Moments later, a rocket-shaped bot blasted skywards. The resulting explosion made the building shudder.

Monica tugged on her strongest boots. "If we don't run for it now, we never will."

Leonard pinched his thighs. "How am I going to do that? My legs are so numb I can barely walk!"

"We'll manage somehow."

Monica gritted her teeth and pulled Leonard to his feet, then slid an arm around his waist. To her surprise, the v-bots moved aside, but they'd not even crossed the living room floor when Leonard slipped from her grasp. He sat on the floor, with v-bots surrounding him.

"You go on," he said in a slurred voice.

Determined not to give up, Monica stamped on several v-bots before unlocking the front door. The corridor thronged with bipedal models, which closely resembled her neighbours, except for their disconcerting lack of clothes. She squirmed and kicked her way through the scrum only to find the elevator out of action and the stairs impassable. The couple from Number 53 shoved her back into the apartment.

She had never liked them.

As she closed the door, a stab of pain in her left ankle demonstrated that leather provided inadequate protection against pincers. A familiar if synthetic-looking cockerpoo growled at her.

"Bad dog," she said.

With numbness climbing her legs, she staggered into the living room, where she found a naked Leonard-alike kneeling on the floor, wielding a dustpan and brush. Evidently, the bots had made quick work of the original.

The man-bot frowned at her. "This place is so dirty."

No longer able to walk, Monica collapsed onto the sofa. A robot voice warbled from the kitchen, "We need more feedstock."

"Duchess" jumped onto her lap. She scratched the dog's plastic ears while awaiting her turn in the recycling hopper.

With the chill seeping into her head, Monica's final thought was that at least her replacement would not have to worry about dust bunnies.

Having trained as an astronomer and subsequently managed an industrial research group, **Vaughan Stanger** now writes SF and fantasy fiction full-time. His short stories have appeared in **Interzone**, **Daily Science Fiction**, **Abyss & Apex**, **Shoreline of Infinity**, and **Nature Futures**, among others, and have been collected in **Moondust Memories, Sons of the Earth & Other Stories**, and **The Last Moonshot & Other Stories**. www.vaughanstanger.com

Art: Siobhan McDonald

The King of China's Mirror

Robert Bagnall

Content Note: Homophobic language, depictions of domestic abuse and chattel slavery

I t's only after John Fisher keeps Wyboston's head underwater for the third time that Wyboston cracks.

"I can't tell you…" he wheezes.

Fisher makes to grab the wires around his wrists, to tip him forward again.

"But I can show you." He's gulping for air.

"No. Tell me."

"I can't explain," he pleads. The bruising around his mouth makes talking difficult. "I can only show you."

"Show me, then."

"I need to take you somewhere. The old clapboard church off the highway."

"The Howling Church?"

He grunts, nods. "You heard it called that too. Untie me."

"Karen?"

The hallway in their little house is uncharacteristically dark and silent. Fisher calls her name again, briefcase at his feet, cursing as he loosens his tie, tightening the knot in the process.

He flicks on the lights in the hall, stares up the stairwell as if something malevolent is waiting for him. Everything is as it should be in the bedroom, her nightgown under her pillow, her toothbrush in its stand in the bathroom, her case on top of the wardrobe. He doesn't know why he thought she packed her things and upped. It's not as if he hit her again. Not really.

He considers the dark, silent kitchen, the pots up on the shelf, an incongruously cheerful cartoon character staring out from a cereal packet. The dark, silent kitchen where Karen should be frying his steak, but instead he's got that damn cartoon tiger, its eyes following him...

He hurls the tumbler at it before he knows what he's doing, watches the Frosted Flakes fall and scatter, watches the glass shatter against the tiles, as if it's somebody else's doing.

He sits in the overly air-conditioned anteroom in his shirtsleeves for an hour staring at the portraits of the Fuehrers: Hitler, Himmler, Doenitz. At the South Carolina Police Department's carved eagle insignia. At its motto in German. When his name is called – as 'Herr Fisher' by a fat woman who follows up by calling him 'John', a combination of toadying to the regime and over-familiarity that makes his blood boil – he has difficulty in hiding his irritation. The police are sympathetic but wary. He gives the same details three times to three different people. He is told to wait forty-eight hours to file a missing persons report. Fisher thought that was only in movies.

"You called her parents?"

"Her father's dead."

"Her mother?"

"No."

"Not dead, or you haven't called."

"Both. Karen's not spoken to her in years."

"Call her."

"Like I say, Karen only has me."

"Mr. Fisher. Please go home and call your wife's mother."

When he summons the courage, it comes as news to her. "How long has she been missing?"

"Two days."

"Two days? Why didn't you call?"

"Because you haven't spoken in years. I"m calling now. Is she there, or isn't she?"

He puts the phone down.

When he next speaks to Calhoun and Lester, the officers assigned, the tone has changed.

"You sure she hasn't just left you?" Calhoun says, adjusting his tie. He's the natty dresser.

"You not giving her what she needs, John?" Lester's technique is to smile while he bullies you, so he thinks you don't notice. "You a fag, John?"

Calhoun follows Lester's lead. "What did you do with her?"

So that's it.

"People say you've got a temper. You got a temper, John?"

"If we find a body you'll be charged."

They think they've shaken Fisher. Only once do they come close, when a figure passes the frosted glass of their door dressed in a long black leather coat. The detectives exchange glances, and then smile grimly at Fisher in unison, the significance clear: one word from them and this all gets passed down the corridor, handed over to the SS.

Fisher knows he's innocent, even if Calhoun and Lester's focus is on proving otherwise. It's down to Fisher to do what they won't: find Karen. His only clue, scrawled in a diary he didn't know she kept, in amongst libelous filth about him that bring grins to their faces: a name.

46

"What's that mean?" Lester asks as Fisher watches them pore over their bedroom.

"Karen kept a diary?"

Lester pushes it closer to Fisher's face. "Is it a person? A place? What? What does it mean? Her last entry, the day she went missing."

Calhoun glances over the page, then at Lester, then at Fisher.

Fisher tells them he doesn't know because he doesn't. It's clear as daylight the gumshoes don't believe him. He stares at the single word on that day's entry, circled and underlined by Karen, his head shaking involuntarily, silently mouthing what's on the page.

Wyboston.

There are five Wybostons in the county phonebook. It's not a common name. A diner, an insurance broker, and three individuals.

Fisher hits the diner on the day and time shown in Karen's diary, pressing her photo at people – "She had her hair shorter" – until the owner reminds him that, yes, he does mind him bothering his clientele. The coffee was all grounds, anyway. You can't get decent coffee since the War.

He discounts the insurance broker: anything financial would have shown up on the radar.

Next, he doorsteps the three local Wybostons figuring he'd catch a look when they saw her photo, heard her name.

"And you say your wife, what? Came here? Called me?"

"Somebody called Wyboston. That's all I know."

"We've family up Fiveways."

"Or it may be a place."

Christopher Wyboston leans on his stick – from his age Fisher guesses at war wounds – and hands back Karen's photo from behind the screen door. "Sorry. But good luck."

As he's walking back to his car, crossing at a junction, wondering how far to cast the net, he sees her, taking her seat and staring through the teardrop window at the Greyhound's rear. She is one of the last passengers and the bus is already pulling away, sliding past, Karen just staring out the window. Her gaze washes over her husband, through him. She registers no surprise or shock, as if he's just another sidewalk stranger.

Karen may not have showed any astonishment, but Fisher's feet stick fast, his eyes bulge, and his jaw drops. Any rate, that's how it feels.

He runs after its receding rear, the bus going through the gears and belching cloying oily smoke. Breathless and defeated, his arms sag. Then he remembers his car is just a block behind.

Ten minutes later he catches sight of the Greyhound, a dozen or so vehicles ahead, at a junction as it turns out into traffic. It dawns on Fisher it's not going to stop before the next town.

He leans on the horn, willing the lights to change. Other drivers glance his way, confused at commotion without cause. Swinging from his lane, he clips a fender. Shouting – all of it directed at him – but he's not listening. Automotive flesh wound, not worth stopping over.

He pushes into traffic. Horns blare. Brakes squeal. He hasn't lost the bus.

He overtakes one, two, three cars, swinging out against oncoming traffic. Lights flash from on-coming vehicles, anger flares from the horns of those behind. But Fisher wants it more.

Luck takes another two vehicles out, ponderously turning off the highway as he leans on the horn to scurry them along. He sweeps past a flatbed and then he's behind the bus, that wall of burnished aluminum with high-set glazing, that gum-smiling advert kid bearing down at him like the Mitchell rear-gunner he once was. He pulls out to get ahead and swerves straight back to the sound of a Mack's air-horn, its banshee wail changing as the rig sweeps past.

Dry-mouthed, he tries again, finding the road ahead clear. Dropping down a gear the car shakes, strains, screams, but he's sliding past the bus, past baffled faces turning to watch.

Out in farmland now, fenced fields, scattered trees, houses and barns built off the highway in the same style. Narrow scrub verges with drainage ditches a yard or two out. No margin for error. Two hundred yards ahead a timber-framed station-wagon wallows out from a farm track and on to the highway, heading straight at him.

It must have seen him, Fisher reasons.

48

It keeps on coming.

Fisher is alongside the bus driver.

The station-wagon keeps on looming.

The Greyhound driver is glaring at Fisher, panicked, angry, incredulous.

Fisher pulls in. Horns blare. He senses rather than sees the station wagon veer, swerve, mount the verge and then fishtail back on to the blacktop. All his focus is on the grille of the bus, the maker's name, in his rear-view mirror.

He brakes.

The bus blares its horn, tries to pull past.

The dull thud-crunch of metal on metal, of vehicle on vehicle, of bus on car, smacks the air from Fisher's lungs. The next thing he remembers is standing at the back of the bus shouting at Karen who stares back at him, mouth agape, eyes confused and terrified, wanting the seat to swallow her up. He knows he's shouting but he can't hear the words. He's pushing the bus driver, a wiry Black man with salt and pepper hair, back towards his seat as he shouts.

It's then he sees the blood, a lot of blood, dripping from his forehead on to the bus floor.

It stops him dead.

He feels curious, hot and cold and clammy. There's a taste in his mouth like he's been licking battery contacts.

He thinks he's going to throw up.

He passes out instead.

It takes a great effort to convince the police who arrest him that they should be talking to their colleagues investigating Karen's disappearance. He's left in an interview room, cold walls painted sallow yellow, high windows with wire-reinforced opaque glass. Just a table, three chairs and Fisher, his head in bandages straight out of a monster movie. He sits and waits, finding it hard to think of reasons not to throw the chairs against the windows.

Calhoun enters, scanning notes in a manila file. Lester follows, wearing a sports jacket. They're halfway through a joke, something about a wristwatch. Fisher is like a distraction to them.

"That was Karen on that bus," Fisher begins, but Calhoun stops him.

"Does your wife speak Serbo-Croat?"

Fisher looks at him like he's gone nuts.

"We had to get a translator. And only after we found out what she was speaking. The woman on the bus speaks Serbo-Croat. And practically no English. She's not Karen."

"That was Karen," Fisher protests, but quietly, his head shaking with disbelief.

"You know what a doppelganger is?" asks Lester.

"Is he in line to be Fuehrer?"

"No, it's your double. And maybe that woman was Karen's double. But it wasn't Karen."

His head hurts. His throat feels dry. He wants to sleep. He wants everything to stop. He doesn't protest, but deep, deep down he knows it was Karen.

"Odd thing," Calhoun adds, with a curious note to his voice, "She thinks it's 1986. And," as if it couldn't get odder, "she says America won the war, and Ronald Reagan is president. She's under observation."

Lester laughs. "I"d ask her where we went wrong, but I can't speak the language."

It was only after he's bailed and released and is cradling a jigger of whiskey in his cold kitchen, that he remembers the blindingly obvious. This Serbo-Croat so-called doppelganger: *she was wearing Karen's dress.* Christopher Wyboston lived just a short walk away from the bus stop where the woman had caught the Greyhound. It was too much of a coincidence.

Through the screen door Fisher sees Christopher Wyboston's face telegraph his train of thought. First, irritation: it's late. Then confusion: Fisher looks familiar, but the dressing around his head obfuscates. He takes a moment to place him. Realization is followed swiftly by sour regret at having shown himself, and an understanding that the game is up. That leaves fear.

That does it for Fisher. That's confirmation. He pulls the screen door open and shoulders his way through the front door, bundles Wyboston down to his own cellar. He doesn't care who's seen him or who else is at home. They'll be dealt with.

Fisher drives. Wyboston sits in the back. His wrists wired to the window-winder, he's no threat.

Wyboston directs them to the derelict church, with its peeling shingled sides, in a wood of willowy trees. The Howling Church. Fisher knows it by sight and reputation but would have missed the hidden turning, particularly in the dark. It's a modest structure, like a model of a church rather than the real thing; a spire that's little more than a dozen or so tapered planks joined like a child's teepee, a space for a window missing its glass. It would have been bright white once, but now the paint's all faded and crumbling, becoming as one with the trees. Nobody would know the church was there unless shown. Or the road, come to that. A hundred yards off the highway and they could have been a hundred miles from other people. Twice Fisher had to get out to pull fallen branches away.

They pull up as close to the building as possible.

"In there," Wyboston says flatly, resigned.

"What is?"

"I need to show you."

"Karen came here?"

"Yes."

"Just you and her?"

"Yes."

"Is she in there?"

"No."

"Then what are you showing me?"

He glares at Fisher, his way of telling him to just go and look at whatever it is.

Fisher snips the wires and, stickless, Wyboston lurches to the steps. By the way he doesn't need to test them for strength, that he knows where to tread, it's obvious he's been here before. Unguided, Fisher fears his foot going straight through rotten wood at any moment.

"Slaves built this," Wyboston says. He leads the way, pushing open doors on hinges that need oiling. Fisher's eyes adjust. He shivers. There's a smell of damp.

Inside are a dozen rows of pews either side of an aisle, angled in to focus on the raised platform. Where a pulpit would normally be, there's a vertical shape instead, like a house door, just standing on its own, covered with a cloth. The one aberration, the one out-of-place object. Wyboston nods towards it.

Fisher sweeps the covering aside. Underneath stands a mirror, the height and width of a man, like in a tailor's shop. Except any respecting tailor wouldn't want one in that condition: faded and chipped, the silver behind the glass foxed.

Wyboston slumps into a pew, staring at Fisher through near-closed eyes, his energy drained. "It's called the King of China's Mirror," he says, as if that explains everything.

Fisher waits for more.

"There was a philosopher called Leibnitz in the seventeenth century. Gottfried Wilhelm Leibniz. He said, suppose there was some way you could become the King of China. Because there was – is – no King of China. But, in his thought experiment, it's not that *you* become the King of China. It's as if there's always been a king, with memories of growing up as a prince, not some sadistic asshole..."

Fisher makes a move.

"You're gonna kill me anyway," Wyboston spits.

"So, there's now a King of China? What's this got to do with Karen?"

"Leibnitz's point was that the situation's exactly the same as if you had ceased to exist and a King of China had just magicked into the world."

Is he mocking me? Fisher thinks. After all he's put him through, has Wyboston led him here as some cosmic joke? "Do you get to be king or not?"

"Leibnitz's argument was that you're you, all the hopes and dreams and memories that make you you. It's a *physical* thing. You can't just be unplugged and slotted into another body. The King of China is the King of China, and you are you. He thought there could be no King of China's mirror. He was wrong. There it is." Wyboston sits back, spent.

Fisher is confused. "So what?"

"It's called philosophy," Wyboston says airily. "I wouldn't expect you to understand."

"And Karen?"

Wyboston considers the mirror warily. "They call this church the Howling Church. It is full of spirits. Souls detached from their bodies, who only now exist in the ether."

"Ghosts?" Fisher's mind is going like two bareknuckle boxers, one trying to work through the logic of mirrors and detached souls, the other pummeling its face in, screaming *what the fuck's this got to do with Karen?*

"That's one name we have for them. I don't know how the mirror came to exist or how old it is. Or by what magic it works. But it allows your soul to slip free into another body and one of the lost souls here to take yours. You become somebody else. You keep your memories and character – your soul, but in another's body, in another era, perhaps even in another place. This is not the only mirror. That is the howling that gives this church its name. The loose souls – the ghosts, to use your word – fighting for your body. Your soul joins them and fights for its own body. I've heard it. Frightful. Brief, but frightful."

Fisher considers the mirror, considers the man. "Did you make all this horseshit up on the drive up, or just since we got in here?"

Wyboston's suddenly petulant, like a child. "Your wife came to me for help. To get away from you. She was panicked. I think its patently obvious why. I didn't wholly believe what she said about you. Now, I think she left a lot out."

"And you're saying she went through the looking-glass, and this Serbo-Croat, this Slav, went the other way?"

"Yes… No. Your wife could be anywhere, any time. *Alternative future. Alternative past.* She may still be in the ether, fighting for a body, or she may have emerged through another mirror in another place. She's not necessarily in the body of the woman whose soul now occupies her body."

Fisher can't contain himself any longer and explodes with laughter. Under the bandages it makes his head hurt. "Have you heard yourself?"

He's more determined than ever that Christopher Wyboston should die, bloodily and slowly, regardless of whether he reveals what happened to Karen. "Even if this were true – which it isn't – why would anybody do this?"

"Because their situation is so desperate, they would do anything to escape." His eyes meet Fisher's. "Like your wife."

That does it. Fisher steps towards him, determined that if he can kill him with one blow, he will.

"You don't believe me?" Wyboston glances at the floor, at the silvery light angling in through the glassless window-frame, at the shadows. "It's almost time."

"Time?" Fisher mocks him to continue.

"When the moonlight strikes the glass…"

"And that's when…"

"Yes. Anybody stood before it…"

Laughing at him, Fisher mimes a vanishing, puff of smoke and all. "And you're asking for the chance to escape, is that it?" he asks. "Prove this horseshit is gospel by playing Alice and going down the rabbit hole?"

Wyboston shakes his head, looks at Fisher like he hasn't been listening. "Not me. It has a greater power than anything you can imagine," he says with fear in his voice.

The moonlight is glinting on the old gilt frame. In a moment it will hit the glass itself. *This will be good*, Fisher chuckles to himself. He'll stand before it and prove it's nothing but a lousy mirror. Then he'll smash it and slice Wyboston open with its shards. He'll wrap his hands with a handkerchief to save cutting himself and slash and stab. Across his arms and face. He'll take his fingers…

He covers his ears, the screaming taking him by surprise, like a punch to the gut when you think you're alone. It's not Wyboston. It's not anyone here. It's everywhere and nowhere, a hollow shrieking, screeching that drops you to your haunches.

When he rises, it's cold. The July heat has gone. The moonlight is now on the opposite side of the glass. How did that happen?

He spins round. No Wyboston. The church is all wrong. The same church, but different. The smell of smoke. Rough hessian mats for knees. A pile of bibles on a shelf. Hymn numbers hanging, white on black.

In the distance, a commotion. Dogs. Men shouting. Coming closer. He looks down.

His hands are black. Small.

His breathing is shallow and scared.

He's wearing a thin shift of grey cotton.

His feet are naked. Small feet.

He looks in the mirror, the same mirror but pristine and clear.

He leans in. His face, wide-eyed. Thin, underfed. Lank hair hanging to his shoulders.

He moves his hands, but they are not his hands. He feels them touching his cheek, but it is not his cheek.

The door bursts open. Men with flaming torches enter, their faces twisted in the flickering light. The muzzles of dogs push between their legs, their growling suddenly loud.

One steps forward. Fisher can't quite believe what he is wearing: a frock coat, necktie and derby hat. He hands his brand to a man behind him, strolls towards the small Black girl that Fisher now is, grinning. He unbuckles his belt and pulls it – slap, slap, slap – through his beltloops.

One of the lynch mob in the shadows laughs, a malicious cackle, anticipating what he knows is about to come.

The man is almost upon Fisher. Fisher instinctively winces. He knows this newcomer has power over him.

"Nancy, you're going to pay this time. Upon my word, you're going to pay. My dogs will eat well tonight."

Robert Bagnall was born in Bedford, England, in 1970. He has written for the BBC, national newspapers, and government ministers. His sci-fi thriller **2084 - The Meschera Bandwidth**, and anthology **24 0s & a 2**, which collects 24 of his sixty-odd published stories, are both available from Amazon. He can be contacted via his blog at meschera.blogspot.com.

The Quality of Life

Louis Evans

I t was a splendid midsummer day, a tawny-golden sousa-phone-D-major toasted-sesame day. Aeron Highsmith walked to work with a spring in his step (¾ time), in his favorite maroon suit (flavors of paprika and rock salt), under a sky whose eggshell blue –when he looked at it –brought a tinkling piccolo to his ears and the taste of matcha tea to his tongue.

Along the way he passed his beloved newsstand and tarried a moment. Its velvet curtains, thick and rich as the last honeyed chords of a sultry coronation waltz, were thrown open to the world. The thirteen bells hanging from its eaves tinkled out cut-crystal notes every color of the rainbow. Aeron paused and plucked a copy of the *Theaportou Times-Gazette*, that noble monochrome publication, and the baroque print in every shade of alabaster, sable, pearl, charcoal, milk and obsidian smiled back at him.

Art: Emily Simeoni

"REVOLT IN THE COLONIES!!!" shouted the headline.

Aeron essayed a small frown. With days as splendid as these, he simply could not conceive what the rebels were so exercised about.

It was another day, a lovely day at the cusp of autumn. The sky outside the office windows was forget-me-not blue and harp concertos, with a flavor so subtle Aeron couldn't recognize it.

Almost *bland*, that taste.

He poured himself a glazed ceramic mug of radiant coffee and sniffed at the cloud of Saturdays that rose above the rim. Delicious.

Lizabet, Aeron's office neighbor, leaned over next to him, inclined like an eroded obelisk, her dress a tapestry of moonlight.

"So how about these qualia shortages, huh?"

"Shortages?"

"It was all over the radio!"

"I never listen to that stuff." The radio programmes were too bright for Aeron, too colorful; and whatever the various scents, they always had a sort of metallic Wednesday aftertaste too.

"So you don't *know*? The rebels blew up six refineries and the big pipeline, and the government says the crisis will all be resolved very crisply now, but there may be some momentary interruptions for the general public. That's why, you know . . ." she pointed out the window with her chin.

"What?"

"You *know*," she repeated, licking her lips theatrically.

Aeron stared out at the sky above the city. Understanding dawned.

"You mean it's flavorless –"

"Shhhh!" A glance over the shoulder, in notes of February and a creaking door hinge. "But, yes. Shortages, you see? Evenly distribute the burden? Everybody chip in to share the load?"

"Good God." In the twenty years since he had moved to the city, Aeron Highsmith had never seen a flavorless sky. Sure, he knew what it was like; he'd grown up in a small town in the provinces where the sky was only flavored on major national holidays and he still visited occasionally –though usually on major national holidays. Hell, back home and in his childhood, there had sometimes been those rolling summer soundouts, when the sky had neither taste nor music, was nothing but a perfect, beautiful color. But that was home. This was the big city: Theaportou, heart of the Empire, home of countless qualia fountains, private and public alike, which imbued every jot and tittle of life with endless sensation. Where the merest scrap of litter would, on closer inspection, ring out with every instrument of an orchestra.

"I'm sure it'll be over soon," muttered Aeron. He felt sullen, even rebellious. He could no longer bear to look up at that tasteless sky.

It was a fine day, half a season onward. The sky was light blue.

The government-provided orchestra gramophones on every street corner blared a patriotic symphony, more or less synchronously. It was loud and brassy and distasteful. It was nothing like the sky had been.

Their tinny melody reached even into the procurator's office where Aeron and Lizabet worked as mid-level clerks.

"Really, we should have the rebels all rounded up and shot," said Aeron. The words surprised him; he never used to say things like that. He'd always been rather tenderhearted about colonial disturbances, he thought. But it felt right.

Lizabet looked at him as though he were a rather stupid child. Her dress was that same shade of silver she always favored, but it didn't look like moonlight anymore. It looked like a dress.

"You don't understand, do you," she said. "We're *losing*."

"But the radio said –"

"The radio *lies*."

"But the army –"

"Shut up and drink your coffee."

He drank. The mug was white, the coffee brown and hot. There were no notes of anything at all.

It was a cold day, months later. Pale sky.

Aeron and Lizabet stood in a long, snaking line.

"But the samizdat digest says we still ship in seventy million kilos a day," said Aeron. "From trading partners. And the strategic reserve."

"That's what I hear," said Lizabet. Her coat had many different baubles on it. They were of different colors and glosses.

"And there's twenty million of us in the city," said Aeron. "So why's the daily ration only half a kilo?"

Lizabet jabbed with her chin in the general direction of the nearby Aldercliffe district, that fashionable (and expensive) neighborhood of skyscrapers and terraced mansions. "It's the private market," she said.

"But the rationing –it's illegal to hoard –" said Aeron. He did not say *what* was rationed, *what* was illegal to hoard. You didn't use those words; not in private, *certainly* not on the ration line. Not unless you wanted violence.

Lizabet shrugged. "It must be *somewhere*."

It was a day. Tens of days later. Blank sky.

Aeron and Lizabet stood in line. It was a very long line now. Since the blockade had begun, even officials and the wealthy had come to stand in the line. The temperature was very low, and there was frozen water everywhere.

Next to them, on the pavement, droned a monk. The monk's prayer was a single nasal syllable, endlessly repeated.

"The monks say, if you meditate, you can sort of . . . make it yourself," said Aeron.

"Can *you* meditate?"

"No."

"Nor I."

It was a very long line. Aeron and Lizabet stood in it. Many seconds passed and they did not shuffle forward. Many seconds passed again.

A truck roared by in the street. It was unmarked and unlabeled, but something about it –the timbre of its engine, the shine of its paint, the bouquet of gasoline –

Aeron *knew. Lizabet* knew.

Everyone in line knew.

The sound that rose up from the line could not be described. Everyone ran after the truck. Its tires squealed as it accelerated, blowing through a stop light and making for Aldercliffe. The mob followed.

The truck was headed for the Mirabaud Manor, and it got there before the mob. But the guards opened the gate too slow.

The mob slammed into the side of the truck and rose up like a wave. The vehicle rocked, toppled –

Slam and the impact burst the back door open, ruptured the leaky tanks within, and qualia tumbled out gushed out sublimed out radiated out and Aeron could *feel* it, the ground-coffee grain of his socks and the badger fur scent of his own sweat and Lizabet's red and furious face glowing like the solstice sunset, and everyone in the crowd could feel the rage and injustice and need that coursed through them like molten brass, like acid and molasses, grabbing the stuff, shoving it in their pockets and in their faces –

And then it was all gone. Used up. Even a truck is a finite volume, much less than the needs of many. Absence rushed in where presence had vanished.

The mob turned. It moved toward the open gate.

And here came the guards now, firing into the crowd, and humans fell, bleeding blank blood onto colorless snow and colorless stones, making loud irregular noises and producing saltwater and bile.

But the mob moved. It took the gate off its hinges and the guards off their feet and trampled them shapeless.

Mirabaud Manor was an old house, built in the days when the rich remembered to fear riots. But it had been rebuilt more recently.

The mob broke down the door.

In the mansion there was *some* qualia –well, a little –just enough to curl gold around the yellow threads of tapestry, to sing a silent octave into the shine of silverware. Not that much.

The mob expanded from room to room, smashing and searching. Old Mirabaud survived in his basement; his niece was not so lucky. The mob found what there was of the qualia, and they took it, and they left.

Nobody took the arts or jewels or metals. They were worthless.

It was another day in spring. The slice of sky visible from the basement where Aeron and Lizabet were hiding was grey.

The rebel troops marching in the street were more disciplined than either Aeron or Lizabet had expected. They wore strange-cut uniforms in unexpected colors.

The radio was speaking of surrender in a muted voice.

There were cans in the basement, and Aeron opened one for their dinner. Despite all his practice, the can slipped. The sharp edge of the can's top struck his inner thumb.

The blood that beaded on his skin did not sing out like trumpets and the pain did not taste like spicy pepper.

But at least it was red.

It was the first day of summer. Aeron and Lizabet were walking through the park.

The provisional government had ended the rationing by ending the rations. That was the rebels' demand, it seemed: an end to qualia extraction. Subjective experience was what you made of it.

And do you know? It seemed, more or less, to work. It wasn't like before, of course; but it wasn't like during, either. Or how it *had* been, Aeron now realized, in the colonies all along. Without the qualia extraction engines running everywhere, everything seemed to have at least a little bit of it to go around. Share the load.

Lizabet's old silver dress was the silver of an old silver dress, not the moon, but in it she still looked quite lovely. And so did Aeron in his prewar maroon suit, for that matter.

Up in the dogwood trees, the flowers were blooming, each the color and scent of a dogwood flower. In the branches sat the larks, and each of them sang with the high, twittering melody of a lark.

Down on the ground, Aeron and Lizabet's hands found each other. They were warm, and soft, and alive. Up above, the sky was an unbroken, flawless shade of sky blue.

Louis Evans is not a doctor of philosophy, but sometimes he makes believe. He is a lifelong, though occasionally lapsed, New Yorker. His work has appeared in **Vice**, **The Magazine of Fantasy & Science Fiction**, **Nature: Futures**, **Analog SF&F**, **Interzone**, and many more. He's online at www.evanslouis.com and in the fediverse at wandering. shop/@louisevans.

Art: James Abel

A

S

h

Jennifer Abell

The Bee Bearer

Lyndsey Croal

E very morning, Eryx roamed the Dry Zone and gathered the bees. Not the healthy ones, of course, but the dead or barely moving, limbs twitching, nectar-desperate kind. This was her job as a Bee Bearer – the most important job in the Colonies, she'd been told during training although, Eryx thought the bees had the most important job.

The first bee she found was nestled in the shade of a rock, its wings flickering a little, still clinging to life. She bent down and offered it a small amount of honey water in her bottle cap – but the bee didn't even have the energy to drink. She sighed, feeling a pang in her chest. It maybe had a few hours left. But there was still something she could do. Hands steady, she picked it up gently so as not to harm the poor creature further.

"Don't worry little bee. We'll get you fixed up. This isn't the end yet." She turned it over and checked for the serial number on the thorax just above the wings. To an untrained eye the markings would look like natural variance, but she could see the distinct patterns in the soft hairs. This one belonged to Apis –the best in the business, and so payment was high for the bees. Eryx smiled and deposited the bee in the box marked 'A' from her satchel. The next bee she found belonged to Apis's competitors, Swarm, and then Hyve. By the end of her walk along the dried-up riverbank, she'd collected eleven bees. A successful day. Well, for her at least, less so for the bees. But it comforted her to remember that they'd be thriving again in the Green Horizon meadows once the City labs took over.

With the bees in her satchel, Eryx began the long march back to town. A drone or two passed her as she walked, probably delivering messages or supplies between Comb City – a place she'd never been – and the towns in the Colonies. It was hot, but it was always hot in the Dry Zone, and sweat tracked down her spine.

Halfway home and parched, she took out her bottle of honey water and dabbed the sweet substance on her tongue, before taking a small sip. She let it sit in her mouth a while, closing her eyes, trying to imagine the flowers and nectar that had made it. It was a hard thing to do when all she'd seen was dust and metal and dying bees. But somewhere on the Green Horizon was the beauty she imagined, just out of reach. Maybe one day she'd get to go there. Occasionally, on gathering mornings, she'd daydream about walking there and returning the bees to the meadows herself. But she'd never be able to save up enough honey water for the journey, and her training forbade it. She had her assigned town and area in the Dry Zone and that was where she'd stay although it wasn't unheard of for other Bearers to leave their colony town, to be replaced days later with the next recruit. Eryx assumed they must have proven themselves good workers and got promoted to a position closer to the City. If she worked hard enough, she might be able to get to the next stage too. Work her way up in the Colonies, to the Green Horizon, maybe all the way to Comb City. Smiling at the thought, she opened her eyes and kept on walking towards the brown horizon, mottled with cracked earth.

Back in town, she went first to the Vendors. Just like the bees, their jobs seemed just as important as hers – they travelled around the Colony towns, gathered the bees from the Bearers and then actually delivered them to the City labs where they were recommissioned, reborn, and sent back to the meadows.

Eryx approached the stall and nodded to the Vendor, Melissa, the one she always brought her gathering to. Melissa lived in the same town as her, so she was familiar, and she always paid her well.

The other woman greeted her with a wave. "How many today?"

Eryx waved back. "Eleven, two for Apis, five for Swarm, four for Hyve."

Melissa's eyes widened. "You know, you're my favourite Bearer in all the Colonies, right?"

Eryx blushed while Melissa signalled to her to empty her satchel. She tipped the individual boxes carefully onto the counter. Some of the bees were still moving – one even tried to crawl across the table. She took a sharp breath. It was difficult to see them this way, but she knew it was for the greater good. Her hand twitched as one of the bees stretched a leg towards the sky as if pointing to something, or as if it had seen the light. Eryx looked up to the hazy sky above it. Someone at training had once told her that in the old stories, bees were thought to be able to fly between life and the afterlife. But Eryx knew there was only one type of life, and that was this one. That was why she did her job, to give the bees another chance at it.

Melissa examined the bees one by one, then smiled. "All in good condition, central system intact. I'll get your units."

As Eryx waited, she reached out a hand to the little bee and touched the outstretched leg. The bee held it there quivering for a few seconds, then its body stilled, and its leg fell. "I hope we'll meet again," she whispered, a tear forming in her eye. Even if it was going to be recommissioned, she didn't like to see it suffer. When she saw the bees so close to the end, she'd have put them out of their misery if that was possible – but then their physical bodies would be too damaged to be brought back and they'd be gone for good. And without the bees, they wouldn't eat. Without them, the Colonies wouldn't survive.

Melissa eventually returned with the units; full payment, enough for supplies and a little extra for her savings. "I'll be putting in a good word for you with the higher-ups as well. You never know, maybe there's a promotion on the horizon," she winked.

Eryx took the payment gratefully. "Thank you, that's very kind."

"Plans tonight?" Melissa asked.

Eryx shook her head. "I'll probably get an early night, all this walking and heat–"

"Makes you tired?" Melissa raised an eyebrow. "You know you tell me that every night."

Eryx tensed her shoulders. Did she really always say that?

"Anyway," Melissa continued. "We're headed to the bar in town tonight if you want to join us?"

"Thank you, I'll think about it," Eryx said. "See you." She waved and walked away, but she knew she wouldn't join Melissa at the bar later. She didn't like mingling with the others. As the only Bearer in this town, she liked to keep to herself. Besides, Bearers' jobs were the most physically taxing, and it took a lot of energy to walk the Dry Zone all day. And the other workers in the Colonies just socialised with their own colleagues – what could she offer in a conversation with some Vendors?

So, she did as she did every evening and headed first to the market, buying a fresh bottle of honey water with her units and some honey cake with what she had left. Then, she went home on her own, ate, and had an early night, ready to rise early the next morning before the midday heat hit. Best if she could get a few hours in before then. Maybe it was her rigid training, her ordered purpose, but Eryx never broke her routine if she could help it.

Later that week, Eryx found twenty-one bees in one haul. When she returned to town and arrived at the Vendor stalls, Melissa was jubilant as Eryx placed the bees onto the counter, one by one.

"That's a new record, kid," Melissa said. "You've got to come for a drink tonight, I won't take no for an answer, okay?"

"I–"

"No *'I'll think about it'*. You're coming. And if you don't show I'll send Juno to come and get you."

Eryx shuddered involuntarily. Juno was the top Vendor, the queen bee of the Colony towns – she was vying for a Comb City promotion and was close to getting it as far as Eryx had heard. She was also twice Eryx's size, and could probably squash her without a second thought if provoked. She gulped. Would it hurt to go for one drink? It could be nice to see more of the town. "Okay then. See you there."

"Oh, and this is for you," Melissa said. "A little extra for good service."

Despite herself, Eryx gasped. Melissa was holding out a flower. An actual flower. Not an artificial one, but a purple one with delicate petals. She took it with a shaking hand and held it to her nose. The scent was sweet, unlike anything she'd smelt before. It was the closest she'd ever got to the Green Horizon. She slotted the flower carefully into the side pocket of her satchel and thanked Melissa. Maybe she'd keep it in water, or better yet, close it in a book and dry it so she could keep it forever.

"Thanks Melissa."

"Thank me by coming for a drink, yeah?"

Eryx took a deep breath and stepped inside the bar, already feeling a little dizzy. A buzz of conversation filled the room, along with the smell of sweat and pheromones. Melissa was at a table with five other Vendors, and she excitedly pulled another chair over when Eryx walked in. The other Vendors eyed her cautiously while Melissa was beaming from ear to ear. Eryx looked around for Juno, but the queen bee wasn't there. Had Melissa exaggerated her influence?

Melissa bounded up to her. "I wasn't sure you'd actually come, my friends didn't believe me when I said I'd got a Bearer to join us for a night out!"

Eryx hesitated at the door. "But... you told me..."

"Come on, I'll get you a drink, what would you like?" Melissa put an arm around Eryx's shoulder and led her to the bar. Eryx could do little to resist although her body prickled with unease. She blinked up at the board, her gut twisting, ears ringing. "I... do they have honey water?"

Melissa roared in laughter and Eryx wished she could sink

into a hole as all eyes of the bar turned to look at her.

"Something funny Mel?" the bartender appeared. When he noticed Eryx his brow creased.

"The *Bearer* asked if you have honey water," Mel said. "It's just," she looked at Eryx as if she was a curiosity, then lowered her voice. "Well, you know."

The bartender looked Eryx up and down and shook his head. "What are you doing bringing a Bearer here, you can't–"

"Don't be prejudiced Carl, why shouldn't she come here? She works just as hard as anyone."

"Harder, I'd wager," Carl said, and Eryx did her best not to make eye contact. "But that doesn't change–"

"How about one of those whisky cocktails, with honey. They say whisky is the water of life so that's basically good, right?" She turned to Eryx who gave a feeble nod. "Or we could take our service elsewhere…"

Carl stiffened. "Sure, Mel, I'll add it to your tab then," he said, and he began to make the drink, though he still eyed Eryx carefully and she shrank under his gaze. Had she done something wrong? She'd never felt tempted to socialise with the Vendors, nor with anyone really, but there was nothing in her training that explicitly forbade it. It was just an accepted part of life in the Colonies that the Bearers kept to themselves, sticking to a rigid routine so they could fulfil their duty. And now she'd broken some convention, and everything seemed out of balance. It was a mistake to come here. She should have just stayed at home. She should go home now. But Mel still gripped her shoulder, and she definitely didn't want to upset her. She was next in line for the top spot if Juno got promoted.

"The others can't wait to meet you," she said brightly, signalling to the table. The Vendors still had their gaze fixed on her – cautious or curious, Eryx couldn't tell.

"Maybe I should go," Eryx said.

Mel softened and squeezed her arm. "Don't be daft, there's no reason you shouldn't enjoy yourself once in a while. And you deserve it after that job you did today," she added, "I can't wait to get those over to the city."

Eryx blanched. "You've not taken them already?"

"Nah, not worth the mileage until I've got a decent amount. Then I take them in batches."

"But some…" Eryx scrambled over the words, feeling light-headed. "Some of them are still alive. They need to be recommissioned as soon as possible."

But Mel only waved her hand. "Ach, the bees won't know the difference. They won't remember this after rebirth, or so I'm told. They have to be retrained, even given a few gene tweaks, then linked back up to the hive, it's a whole process."

"But they still suffer."

"Look kid, this is how we all do it." She motioned to her friends behind her. "You won't find a single Vendor that goes to the City with only a few bees. Otherwise no one here would make enough profit, and we'd never have a chance of leaving this desert. You're doing your job, your duty, by saving them for rebirth, don't worry beyond that."

Eryx was about to argue that the bees' wellbeing should be more important than their own personal profit, but Mel shoved the drink into her hand and she lost any confidence she had left. Instead, she peered over the edge of the glass and sniffed it. There was the distinct sweet smell of honey but there was also something else – something smoky. She took a small sip, and then another. The drink was unlike anything she'd ever tasted. It warmed her throat. It didn't take her long to begin to feel dazed, and when Mel led her over to the table, she didn't complain.

When Mel asked her to recount how many bees she'd saved this week, she just drank up and told them. The other Vendors seemed fascinated by what she was saying, nodding along and occasionally flashing a smile at Mel who seemed energised, cocky – the queen bee of this particular group.

When one of them asked to see her symbol, the small tattoo on her wrist, Eryx rolled up her sleeve and let them gawk. Everyone got the tattoo during training; it was a rite of passage. Hers had an 'A' marked on it, for authorised, she assumed.

"–seen one up close," one of Mel's friends said, though Eryx had missed the first part of the sentence in the smoky haze of whisky.

"I can't believe they actually brand them," another added. Had they moved on to a new conversation?

"They're a valuable commodity," Mel said, smiling at Eryx. They must be talking about the bees. Eryx smiled back, and when her drink was finished, Mel handed her another.

Eryx woke up with a thrumming in her ears. Something wasn't right. She sat bolt upright on her cot and looked out the window. It was already after dawn. Her heart began to race. She'd never been late to her work, her duty, and it set off a chain reaction of panic and adrenaline. She leapt up and scrambled to get ready, packing everything quickly into her satchel. Then, she headed out into the Dry Zone.

The first hours of walking were a slog, and already the morning sun felt scorching on her body. She reached into her satchel for her water bottle, but her hand only found empty air. She must have left it in the bar the night before. Her throat suddenly felt very dry. She should go back. But if she did, she'd have nothing to show. No bees, no pay. She'd probably manage a day or two without, but some days were slow and she liked to have savings stored, just in case. And any bees she missed today could die or get damaged in overnight sandstorms or the cold. No, she'd go and just gather what she could, then come back early.

A few hours later she was parched, while a crushing headache was making her dizzy. And, despite drinking so much the night before, she was thirstier than she'd ever been. The drink Mel had given her must not have been the hydrating kind. The night itself was a haze – she hadn't really felt like herself with the vendors, being around them put a fog in her mind. She cursed herself for changing her routine, and now she was tired and potentially out of pocket. She looked down at the path and stopped suddenly, jerking up her foot as she almost stepped on a bee. She moved back and crouched down to it, narrowing her eyes as the ground wobbled. It was barely clinging to life, the kind of bee she'd have usually given honey water to, and sent on its way because there was still hope it could make it back to Green Horizon. She checked her satchel, in case she'd missed the water bottle earlier but it was no use. She looked around, panic descending like a swarm. No one but her here – this was her area after all. If she left the bee here, it would die slow. If she took it home, it might die slow too, boxed up until Mel thought she had enough of them to take to the city. The thought of the poor bees, half dead in the little boxes for days on end brought on another wave of nausea. For the first time since she'd started her job, she was unsure how to fulfil her duty.

The options tugged at her like not enough honey spread over dry toast. And then something else tugged at her. A feeling in her chest, as if she'd been stung suddenly in the heart and it was stretching out now over her body. The feeling was almost familiar, euphoric. She fell into the dust, her limbs twitching.

This is it, she thought. *This is how it ends.* And the bee would watch her, and she would watch it, together at the last. She reached out her hand to the bee and, seeming to understand, the creature crawled into her hand. Its body vibrated gently in her palm.

"Sorry little bee," she said, wishing she was closer to the Green Horizon. "I don't have any nectar." But then she remembered the flower – the one Mel had given her. She reached slowly for her satchel and pulled out the flower from the side pocket. A few of the petals were damaged, but the flower itself was still whole. Maybe it would be enough, she placed it on her palm and watched as the bee moved towards it. After a few moments, tongue extended, it drank. Long seconds passed, then the bee brushed its body with its legs as if preparing to fly. Eryx looked for the serial number. Maybe it was her eyes fading, but she couldn't see one, and before she could bring it closer to look properly, the bee had flown away, disappearing into the vastness of the Dry Zone.

As Eryx lay dying, she strained to turn her head to look across the landscape. Just on the horizon stretched a wall of green, where the bees were supposed to be. Sometimes, they flew off their path. Sometimes too far. She stared at the Green Horizon, wishing she could see it up close. Just once. Instead, she closed her palm around the purple flower as her eyes welled.

There was a noise from nearby. A buzz of wings. A staccato whirr. For a second, she imagined the bee had come back, but it was just a drone, the kind that transported larger cargo to Comb City. It flitted above her and prodded her with one of its mechanical limbs. Then, it turned over her arm and flew down close to inspect her wrist. "Don't worry Eryx," its monotone voice said. "We'll get you fixed up. This isn't the end yet." And then it picked her up and she was flying, her body limp.

She soon realised the drone was taking her towards the meadows, and she fought to keep her eyes open, to see it before everything went dark. As she whirled over the Green Horizon, she had a strange feeling she'd been here before, like she'd seen it in her dreams. Bees trilled in harmony amongst brightly blooming flowers and she could taste a burst of sweetness in the air. With her last breath, she let go of the purple flower.

Crushed petals fell like teardrops to the meadows below.

Lyndsey is an Edinburgh-based author of strange and speculative fiction, with work published in several magazines and anthologies. She's a **Scottish Book Trust New Writers Awardee, British Fantasy Award Finalist**, former **Hawthornden Fellow**, and a **LOHF Writers Grant Recipient**. Her debut novelette **Have You Decided On Your Question** is published in April 2023 with Shortwave Publishing. Find her on Twitter as @writerlynds or via her website lyndseycroal.co.uk

On the anniversary of the abdication

Townes-Thomas

Stale rituals
       that day
when the big president is
raised
from his nursing

bed.   I sought
out a cemetery
where a first-pod
had fallen. Finding
a crater

       among gravestones
pre-dating the great
signing-over, I chanted
a homemade psalm
in the fog —

a prayer to counter
the unsung song
      of the age.
Weak lament rose
and filled the crater

for a while, seeming —
once sung —
to settle   on
the moss and soil
as if

scanned
      and disassembled.
In such silence
had the first-pods
deciphered prophecy

from garbled
talk-shows and newscasts
hurled nightly
      into the void
by our satellites.

Now a wordless alien canticle
shows to synapses
      the expanse

      of space,

screaming.

And earth
sings
      eternal and forever
crumbling in cemetery
mist.

Reformation

Townes-Thomas

and as is normal,
the latest class of trainee
teachers — as guardians
of our science, leaders of
reformation — swallow
hallucinogens and sink
into the gallery of frag
-ments. Too soon, one
of them enters

a Benandanti vision
of sorghum and fennel;
learns poisoned wine
disorients; soon begs
for water

at the village. Another
— sleep-paralysed — is
frightened trying
to disaggregate
some fin de siècle
occultism, it
liquid slips through
her fingers, bending
and shaping contra gravity
and perspective;

a banshee howls
in her ear. Meanwhile,

a young bloke bashes
a misheard Kalahari
bush poem with 21st

century atheist
blogpost — sheds tears
when it declines
to break. But

all in the end do learn, common
senses on fire, just
to sit and look
at the quenching
blaze. The colours
compete, and the eyes
don't blink, the spines
are alive, and the skin is
alive. And vocation burns
in the chest.

Townes-Thomas lives a quiet life in London, England, and spends his time struggling to make sense of the things he reads, and the world in general. Some of his haibun are forthcoming in **Scifaikuest**.

Elegy for the Midden Wife
Amelia Gorman

Her best dress is for the wrong season
the Company Town rarely sees winter
more often beset by a warm rotten rain
I don't know if she or the town has a name

that can go on slabs that will mark both graves.
Hers today, I will close the plastic casket
after I pick the pieces of wire and hair
from her moth bitten wool sleeves.

Her hands that have been bled by pins
and beer bottles will never see another life
into the world, and so her mantel passes to
woodcarvers, or sourdough fermenters.

She made children from the streets, made them better
than others because she made them out of nothing
at all, nibbles from the butcher, rotten fat,
ribs — no child ever had the same number.

In a town with so many wasted bodies,
in Teratogen County, she made smiles from nothing,
She made fairy tale pistil children, the snow whites
for blackened insides, every body here changed

by the Mine, Smelter, Sifter, but she coaxed life
out of waxed paper and protein bar wrappers and breathed
a little cough into leather strap lips and cellophane lungs,
worked the chicken bone legs until they could stand and run.

Laughter outside drowns out the deliveries and trains,
goes on through the caustic rain and withering wind.
Her wake is empty except for me, her life ripples out.
Her dirty children play in the streets in all seasons.

"Elegy for the Midden-Wife" is a reprint, first published in Star*Line.

The Little Spider Mermaid

Amelia Gorman

After also coming out of the ocean,
you said it hurts to dance on two feet.
Try eight knives, balancing on eight blades,
eight blue streaks of blood on the ballroom floor;
a thing worth having two of is worth having more.
And the kingdom nears, and the tide fades.
And I'm left with just the bold deceit
of my new symmetry in motion.

After my awkward crawl from the sea
post-deal with the hagfish, for eight new legs
and gaudy silks to grow and to wear and a hunger,
a curiosity regarding why no one finds it weird: why men
still swarm around me, why men yet kneel before me when
I am sticky with my ribbons and lace. I tongue their
meat, while the pulsing package inside me begs
for escape, to eat, to spin huge and free.

If it's worth having two, it's worth eight.
If it's worth eating a little, it's worth eating a lot.
If I have the chance to gain some hunger at the cost
of my soul, I will make that hard wager at the hagfish's table.
Stretch out my new limbs, segmented & sharp & dewy & able,
never look back at the tides or the tail that I've lost,
instead across the kingdom at the prey I caught;
and I gorge, I barter, I multiply, I create.

Amelia Gorman is a recent transplant to Eureka, California and you
can usually find her walking her dogs or foster dogs in the woods or
exploring tide pools. Her fiction has appeared recently in Nightscript
6 and is forthcoming in **Cellar Door** from Dark Peninsula Press. Read
some of her recent poetry in **New Feathers** and **Vastarie**n. Her first
chapbook, **Field Guide to Invasive Species of Minnesota**, is available
from Interstellar Flight Press.

Tamales on Mars

Angela Acosta

The dry soil of Mars could be
the deserts of Chihuahua,
Bolivian salt flats
or the frigid Patagonian steppe.

Here, my bisabuela's recipes
can find new homes
with ingredients harvested
and cooked underground.

Pottery wheels hum in time
with the wind, birthing
new cooking vessels
in gritty, red stoneware.

We make tamales on Sundays,
filling them with the sweets
of dried fruits left in the sun
and cheeses from goats happily
jumping in Martian gravity.

The taste compares to Terran delights.
We eat tamales and protein rich beans
around a roaring fire where colonists
tell stories of skies of blue
and arid deserts like these.

"Tamales on Mars" was first published in *Sprawl Magazine* (2022)

Extrasepulchral

Angela Acosta

A sepulcher cannot be built in space,
only flown as the comfortable onboard habitat
will give way to vacuum, a sterile burial.

An airlock breech elicits a last breath
just beyond the tomb of vapid vapors
released by the skeleton crew of the ship.

She lurches forwards, gulping atmosphere,
churning through the froth of the edge of space,
hurtling past the space station where oxygen ignites.

Death in space is merciless, untamed,
explosively calm as our bodies return to atoms,
nearly immortal while our organic selves dissolve.

Terrans and those from beyond the solar system
still worry about the dalliances of home worlds,
the ideal lives of feet placed firmly on artificial gravity.

The velocity of the crash landing hasn't caught up
with the cultural norms of death and burial rights,
no time for final words to slip from frozen lips.

One can only witness such devastation,
our psychologies and the human eye could never see
what extrasepulchral catastrophes the future will bring.

Angela Acosta is a bilingual Latina poet and scholar with a passion for the distant future and possible now. She won the 2015 **Rhina P. Espaillat Award** from West Chester University, and her work has or will appear in **On Spec, Penumbric, MacroMicroCosm,** and **Eye to the Telescope.** She is author of **Summoning Space Travelers** (Hiraeth Books, 2023) and the forthcoming chapbook **Fourth Generation Chicana Unicorn** (dancing girl press, 2023). She is currently completing her Ph.D. in Iberian Studies at The Ohio State University and resides in Columbus, Ohio.

Video Performance

Alliance Rising

CJ Cherryh & Jane S Fancher
Daw Books, January 2019
Review by Phil Nicholls

Alliance Rising is the first in the Hinder Star series, which means it is part of Cherryh's classic Alliance-Union world. While there are already many books set in this universe, the Hinder Stars series tells the backstory of this amazing setting.

The book recounts significant events in the history of the Hinder Stars, those stars closest to Earth. The story begins when the merchant ship Finity's End arrives at Alpha Station. The Captain of Finity's End invites the local merchant families into the new Merchanter Alliance. However, the Sol authorities on Alpha do not react well to either the arrival of the massive Finity's End or the proposed alliance of merchant ships.

The presence at Alpha of a similar-sized ship which is being built by Sol further complicates the situation. When the Alpha-based merchanters realise that this new ship is not configured to carry cargo, the dispute quickly escalates. If Sol is building a warship, then this could be a prelude to war with those stations further out in human space.

These political machinations form the backdrop to events on Alpha docks, where local merchanters and the crew of Finity's End mix. Ross and Fallon, crew of the local Galway, are quickly caught up in the tensions, drawn to side with the visiting spacers, yet wanting to support their home station. These personal conflicts run parallel with the wider plot.

For a book written by two authors, the tone and style of *Alliance Rising* is seamless. Frankly, this reads just like any other CJ Cherryh SF novel I have read. With all due respect for Fancher, Cherryh is the more prolific writer, so it is not surprising that her style shines through the novel.

In her previous work, Cherryh excels at making emotional or political conflicts as thrilling as a battle. *Alliance Rising* is no different, where events and bad choices ratchet up the situation on Alpha's docks. Yet, this is the first book in a new series, so do not expect the plot to be neatly wrapped up by the end. There is a story arc, but much remains unresolved. *Alliance Rising* effectively lays the groundwork for the next book in the series.

I loved reading about the origins of the Alliance-Union setting and learning more about the Neihart family who run Finity's End. For anyone familiar with Cherryh's SF universe, *Alliance Rising* was a wonderful combination of the new and the familiar. Finity's End has a novel to itself later in the series, so *Alliance Rising* was like reading the family history of an old friend.

Yet, the book also works as an introduction to the complex Alliance-Union setting. Here we are during the establishment of the merchanters who are a staple part of the setting. *Alliance Rising* is an ideal way to

sample the world of the Alliance-Union, with a book that takes a fresh look at this classic hard SF universe.

Alliance Unbound, Part 2 of The Hinder Stars series is scheduled for publication in August 2023.

The Midnight Circus

Jane Yolen
Tachyon Books, 2020
Review by Duncan Lunan

In *The Jungle Book*, and also in his anthology *Twenty-one Tales*, Rudyard Kipling follows each story with a relevant poem. They're all effective, and 'Jane's Marriage', which follows 'The Janeites' in *Twenty-one Tales,* has a showstopper of a first verse which I'm having to force myself not to quote here, when reviewing the work of another Jane. *The Midnight Circus* also has a poem to accompany each story, but they're collected at the end of the book, along with notes on the stories, robbing the poems of the chance to make a similar impact. In reviewing them together here I'll have to jump to and from the appendices, which I hate doing, but I think it's necessary. For example, 'The White Seal Maid' and its 'Ballad of the White Seal Maid' (which has been set to music elsewhere) are both simple retellings, lyrically written, of the basic selchie legend – without the tragic, foreshadowed ending of the traditional ballad *Sule Skerry*. The characters will never be reunited, but the story and the poem would be happier together, not 184 pages apart. 'Winter's King' and the poem 'If Winter' have similar structures, with the changeling boy drawn fatally to forest and ice rather than to the sea. 'The Fisherman's Wife' and its poem 'Undine' tell much the same story about a mermaid, but the Notes are prefaced, 'I like strong women', and in the story the heroine gets her man back from the sea and the mermaid's clutches.

'Become a Warrior' features another archetypal strong woman: the daughter who survives the conquest of her kingdom, and lives first in disguise and then in the wild while waiting for her revenge. Jane Yolen's Notes say that this one started as a very different story (I keep thinking of Lessa in Anne McCaffrey's *Dragonrider)*, but what started as 'a positive, uplifting story' for an anthology called *Warrior Princesses*, 'went darker, and then darker still'.

'The House of Seven Angels'

and its poem 'Anticipation' retell another traditional story, this one from Yolen's own Jewish background. In her preface, 'Who Knew I Was a Writer of Dark Stories?', Jane Yolen half-apologises for finding that there were so many of them when she put this collection together, but 'The House of Seven Angels' isn't one of them. Similarly, 'Night Wolves' and its poem 'Bad Dreams' are about a growing boy beating the terrors of a house in darkness, be they real or imagined, and the story ends happily.

'The Weaver of Tomorrow' is set in that fantasy world which I've characterised elsewhere as 'England before the Black Death' (and with magic that actually works). Like the Norns, the Lady of Shalott, and the hostage of Glun the Unavoidable in Jack Vance's *The Dying Earth*, the Weaver's tapestry not only portrays but determines the present and the future, including her own death – and when it comes, someone must take her place. The poem, 'The Wheel', describes the process.

When I was in New York, the thing that amazed me about Central Park was the number of people there after dark, thronging the pavements if not the areas between. I mentioned it to my taxi driver, who replied that he didn't understand it either: "If the car breaks down, I'll just wind up the windows and wait until daylight". 'The Wilding' (taking the name of a real-life gang) is about the underlying violence, wrapped up in a story of shape-changing, but the real killer is an unchanged human, and the poem is about the innocence of being an animal. The story and the poem have a lot in common with their counterparts, 'Great Gray' and 'Remembering the Great Gray', which struck a chord with me because I've twice had memorable experiences with big owls in the USA. 'Dog Boy Remembers' is another variation on the same human-into-animal theme, a precursor to a story and novel published elsewhere.

'Requiem Antarctica' (a collaboration with Antarctic expert Robert J. Harris) has the premiss that Captain

Scott was a vampire, and Oates took to the ice rather than continue to feed him. It's a great idea, and very well written, as is the poem, but it's not too easily reconciled with Scott's dying wish for his son Peter: "Teach the boy natural history, it is better than games". That would sit better with 'Deer, Dances', the poem which follows 'The Wilding'. 'Little Red' and its poem 'Red at Eighty-one' have themes similar to both 'The Wilding' and 'Requiem Antarctica', but the twist is that they're alternative versions of 'Little Red Riding Hood.'

'Inheritance' is prefaced and supposedly inspired by a poem on one of the Callanish stones, on the island of Lewis. but there's no mention of it in the Notes. Jane Yolen's poem is about the stones, but there's little about them in the story, which is about a Hebridean love-charm which goes wrong and leads to murder.

'An Infestation of Angels' is one of the most unusual stories in the book. The twist is that the last plague in Egypt, persuading 'the Faró' to let The People go, is a blight of cannibalistic angels with other unclean habits. The Notes relate it only to the Exodus, but there is another, possibly related myth. The Red Sea, where 'Pharaoh's army got drownded', in the words of the spiritual, and where The People are heading at the end, was where the angels Senoy, Sansenoy and Semangelaf had their confrontation with Lilith, Adam's first wife, who had become a vampire with a particularly evil power over male children – as the ones here carry off the two firstborn sons of the Faró. If the angels in the myth hadn't subdued her, the angels in this story could well be her offspring.

'The Snatchers' by contrast is set in the real world of Tsarist Russia, with its indifference to the plight of Jewish boys conscripted into the army, and the mutilations inflicted by their parents trying to save them from that. There's a supernatural element to the Snatchers, who colluded with the authorities to abduct boys before they could be made unfit to serve, and they have resurfaced in 1960s America to force pacifists into the Vietnam war. But what it's really about, as the poem implies, is the effect on the parents. 'Names', the last story in the book, is another post-Holocaust story, a simple account of surviving children who have memorised the names of the dead, rather like the talking books of *Fahrenheit 451*. Its poem, 'What the Oven Is Not', is one of the shortest poems in the book, and the most powerful of them.

To sum it up, the stories are compelling, the poems are good – some of them excellent – and the book is well worth reading. But just to say it again, the poems belong with the stories, to back up their messages, and not tucked away at the end of the book, which would work much more effectively if they had been printed together.

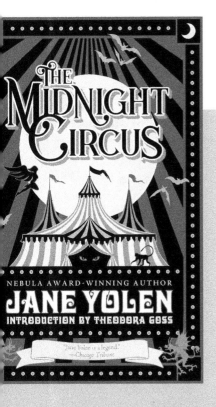

The dark imaginings of fantasy icon Jane Yolen are not for the faint of heart

Barzakh: The Land In-Between

Moussa Ould Ebnou; Translated by Marybeth Timmermann

Iskanchi Press, October 2022

Review by Veronika Groke

Mauritanian novelist Moussa Ould Ebnou's science fiction novel *Barzakh: The Land In-Between* takes the reader on an epic journey through space and time. In an unknown distant future, researchers from the Archaeological Institute of Human Thought manage to extract memory transcripts from an ancient skeleton buried on top of Ghallawiya mountain. Starting in an eleventh-century desert village and ending in the fictitious Republic of Barzakh of the 2050s, these memories tell the story of Gara, a young man abducted into slavery by travelling salt merchants, and his struggle to escape what he increasingly perceives to be the inherent evils of humanity.

Since Gara's death is established at the beginning, the entire novel is basically a flashback – or rather, a series of flashbacks that takes us through three distinct time periods separated by the narrator's near-death experiences. Taking its name from a Muslim concept denoting a place between life and death where souls gather before going on to the afterlife, *Barzakh* is very much a book in-between: set in a geography comprised of both real and (semi-)mythic places, and incorporating elements from Mauritanian history and Islamic tradition alike, the story jumps between science fiction, historical fiction, and dystopian narrative, thereby reflecting the narrator's increasing inability to know himself.

That Gara is not the most reliable of narrators becomes clear pretty soon: for all his introspection and pondering on humanity's corrupted nature, there are some remarkable blind spots in his perception. While he personally resents his own enslavement, the idea that slavery as an institution may be wrong only arises when it is suggested by others. The stoning of a young bride in one of the villages the caravan stops at is merely background noise, and at no point does it occur to Gara to

Barzakh: The Land In-Between

a novel

Moussa Ould Ebnou

Translated by Marybeth Timmermann

question whether the cruelty with which the caravan men treat their animals might also be morally questionable. On the other hand, sequences such as Gara's surprisingly detailed imagining of what the caravan leader is thinking about when he starts lagging behind at some point (i.e., the many creative ways he could take revenge on his wife, whom he suspects of being unfaithful to him) alert us to the fact that this is a book in which reading between the lines is as important as what is actually being said.

Throughout the novel, it is intriguing what is left out and what is described in detail. When, after a long and arduous journey, Gara's caravan reaches the city of Ghana, which he says had 'always fascinated' him, his stay there is quickly skipped over with little more information than that they 'stayed [there] for three weeks.' In contrast, the novel abounds in detailed descriptions of the desert landscapes the protagonist passes through, some of which are achingly beautiful. This is a landscape 'carved... by the light and wind', in which people measure the time by the length of shadows, and shadows themselves almost behave like people, stretching out 'lazily', 'caressing' the sand. Destinations, it turns out, are not where the story is at; rather, this is a book that is all about the journey.

Torn between his loathing of his fellow people and a deep longing for a more meaningful connection both with them and with the unconscious parts of himself that remain hidden from him, Gara is, however, ultimately unable to enjoy the ride. Seemingly unclear himself whether what he is seeking is solitude or a better humanity, he keeps circling back on himself, watching his former potential futures turn to myths of the past, encountering people and places that, though separated by centuries, remain strangely reminiscent of one another.

Though acutely aware of my own shortcomings as a reader in this case (I had never read any African science fiction before, and my ignorance of Islamic tradition is considerable), I found *Barzakh* to be an enjoyable read. This was not least due to the originality and beauty of the descriptive passages (masterfully rendered into English by translator Marybeth Timmermann). Admittedly, though, they tend to be rather lengthy, so if fast-paced and action-packed is what you like, *Barzakh* may not be the book for you. To all those who do have the patience, I would recommend to dive in and expect the unexpected.

----------------------------------- →

In *Shoreline*, we're keen to promote the work of SF authors who are not so well known in the Anglophone world. Here, we showcase the work of the Mauritanian author Moussa Ould Ebnou who has written several novels and short stories in both French and Arabic. Ebnou's novel *Barzakh* was written in French and first published in Paris in 1990, before being translated by the author himself into Arabic and published as *Madinetou al-riah*. Now it has been translated into English by Marybeth Timmermann and published by Iskanchi Press as *Barzakh: The Land In-Between*.

Barzakh is described as 'a blend of science fiction and philosophy, an innovative masterpiece that symphonizes mysticism, religion, and Mauritanian culture into a dystopian reflection on the human condition.' In this article, Ebnou introduces the themes in *Barzakh* and explores the influences upon his work.

— Pippa Goldschmidt

A Textual Analysis of

Barzakh: The Land In-Between

Moussa Ould Ebnou

I write science fiction because I'm not happy with this world and, as Philip K. Dick said, 'If you are not happy with this world, seek another world.' I would say, quoting Heinlein and Asimov, that science fiction is 'speculative fiction', a 'branch of literature concerned with human responses to advances in science and technology.'

Influence of Tradition

Barzakh, in its first and second parts, recalls periods of the past; through its hero Gara, who is a time traveller from the eleventh century to the twentieth century, thanks to the Green One who guards the sea of time and transports him to show him what humankind will become. I have inserted ancient tradition into this science fiction novel, through Greek philosophy and tragedy and through the Mauritanian folk music tradition.

A symphonic novel

Barzakh is structured like a concert of Moorish lute music which consists of three ways, the black way, the white way and the speckled way. In the novel, this becomes the Milky Way which, according to Moorish musical mythology, was invented by a ghoul, a non-human. This third part of the novel introduces extra-terrestrial characters and takes place when part of humanity has left Earth for other planets. Each part of the novel consists of five chapters and a prelude which consists of each of the voices of the lute. This intertextuality between the parts and chapters of the novel and the ways of the lute, highlight the common nature of the narrative time and the musical time, because literature and music simulate the same time, that of myth. *Barzakh* is therefore a symphonic novel in the proper sense.

A narrative dilemma

The Qur'anic stories help me solve the narrative dilemma of an instant in which Gara revisits his entire life that spanned ten centuries: It has been stated in the Holy Qur'an, in Surah Qaf, that this instant exists, and it is the moment of the throes of death:

(وَجَاءَتْ سَكْرَةُ ٱلْمَوْتِ بِٱلْحَقِّ ذَٰلِكَ مَا كُنتَ مِنْهُ تَحِيدُ (19) وَنُفِخَ فِي ٱلصُّورِ ذَٰلِكَ يَوْمُ ٱلْوَعِيدِ (20) وَجَاءَتْ كُلُّ نَفْسٍ مَّعَهَا سَائِقٌ وَشَهِيدٌج (21) لَّقَدْ كُنتَ فِي غَفْلَةٍ مِّنْ هَٰذَا فَكَشَفْنَا عَنكَ غِطَاءَكَ فَبَصَرُكَ ٱلْيَوْمَ حَدِيدٌ (22) وَقَالَ قَرِينُهُ هَٰذَا مَا لَدَيَّ عَتِيدٌ (23))

The moment of agony came, and all the truth was revealed. [19] This is the Day `you were` warned of.[20] Each soul will come forth with an angel to drive it and another to testify.[21] You were totally heedless of this. Now we have lifted this veil of yours, so today your sight is sharp.[22] Here are the records ready.[23]

When the death throes arrive, time stretches to turn around, so the beginning is recalled and the truth unfolds. The story narrates this moment of truth, the moment of death, in which the past life of the dying is revealed. At this moment the hero narrates, with insight, events he lived through in a time that spanned ten centuries, judging them with insight:

"...Throughout my existence, I have always tried in vain to

90

connect my life to my dreams, my conscious to my unconscious, and my consciousness to other consciousnesses, so that I could judge others, myself, and time with cool composure. But I remained isolated, a simple monad - adjusted, protected, and absolutely cut off from everything else. And suddenly now, at the moment of my death, all these connections automatically formed with no effort on my part. In the throes of death, my dream and my life descended before me into the arena to be given an ultimate explanation, lining up in one very straight line, before sinking into the void. The entire world was piled up in a sort of little circular and transparent porthole, located just in front of me, where all enigmas and all secrets had come to be resolved and became self-evident. The past, the present, and the future had merged together into a single instant. Dying had shed its unremitting light into every corner of my life, laying bare everything I had touched. I suddenly discovered the hidden meaning of situations, the significance of each silence, every gesture and spoken word. Nothing about any being or thing escapes me now, not even their intentions. My entire life – so close, so inaccessible, and so inordinately gratuitous – was rewound and then replayed before me, a washed-up actor, an immobile spectator this time, tormented by the profound regret of having participated in this grotesque comedy..." (*BARZAKH: The Land In-Between*, pp 10-11).

The semantics of the names

When I write, I translate, I try to spread a new reality in language and terminology that transcends the rules of reception and acceptance, to produce a text that suggests new meanings of places, times, people, and terms. This translation produces new meanings that are not found in any list of terms or in any language, and leads to musical ecstasy and refers to metaphysics. The deviation of these meanings is evident when creativity crosses the borders of languages. Thus, with the name of one of the characters, Ghostbuster, is designed to sound like Aoudaghost, I go beyond languages to get to the heart of the meaning of this character's function in the novel.

The word Ghostbuster becomes the name of the head of the archaeological expedition that searches for Aoudaghost, the lost caravan city, which was buried by sand, and no one knows where it is. Three words were formed according to their sound, 'Ghost', 'Buster' and 'Aoudaghost' (the name of the caravan station lost in the desert) - so that 'Ghostbuster' becomes the name of the archaeologist in the novel, whose name means in English, 'ghost seeker'...

My literary bilingualism

Barzakh was first written in French. For me, as for many foreign language writers, bilingualism is a legacy imposed by colonization. My use of French as a language of writing is explained by the fact that, in my country, I was educated in a French school. At first, I wrote only in French, but after the publication of this novel, I opted for literary bilingualism by self-translating my books already published in French into Arabic. Reading the two versions, French and Arabic, one wonders in which first language they were written, and one no longer knows which version to consider as the principal part. In fact, we find ourselves before a triptych whose central section is the initial unwritten version (isn't every text the translation of an ideal text existing only in the mind of its creator, who then 'puts it into words' in one or more languages?) and the side panels, the French and Arabic versions. This self-translated version gives me the opportunity to find my mother tongue and, despite the complex work of the translation, I become more spontaneous in Arabic and recover authenticity. I translate myself in order to tame my linguistic duality. Self-translation, or parallel creation, can then appear as a way of transcending the split, of reconciling the two halves of the internally torn being, by making the two languages coexist harmoniously.

I have often wondered why I write in French and then translate into Arabic. I would say, following Beckett, that "my own language appears to me like a veil that must be torn in two to reach the things (or the Nothingness) which are hidden behind." By writing first in French, I seek to distance myself from what is familiar to me by distancing myself from my language. French, the foreign language, is a necessary tool to get rid of the rhetoric of the Arabic language and escape the conventions, automatisms and expressions of the mother tongue.

SF as speculative fiction is philosophical.

I am a professor of philosophy, and I write science fiction like a philosopher who reasons by myth or like a mathematician who reasons by the absurd! SF as speculative fiction is philosophical. Like Platonic myths, those of science fiction can save us, if we believe them. The myths of SF reveal what was hidden from us from the start. My fiction is rooted in human anxieties in the face of the techno-scientific present, but also in hope and wonder. Today, the borders between SF and mainstream are no longer very precise, especially with respect to novels.

SF Africa, a Copernican revolution

SF can contribute to the development of African thought by transforming its methods and ideas. It can help Africans transform their mentalities to support changes and harmonize their development models. SF can produce a true Copernican revolution in African thought, and a change of perspective in that thought. In Africa, we tend to look to the past to inform our present, whereas SF can help Africans look to the future to understand their present. The stakes of the future being already in the present, SF can help produce a backward reflection that illuminates the present through the future. Another world is being built, and SF can help Africans understand and inhabit it.

Moussa Ould Ebnou, one of Mauritania's greatest novelists, earned his Ph.D. at the Sorbonne in Paris, France, and is a philosophy professor at the University of Nouakchott in Mauritania. He has written several novels and short stories in French and Arabic. He was a consultant for the United Nations Sudano-Sahelian Office in New York and served as a cultural advisor to the Presidency of Mauritania for fifteen years.

Noise and Sparks

Ruth EJ Is Unwell

Ruth EJ Booth

I get MIGRAINES.

My MIGRAINES are usually pretty LOUD and RED.

This time is different.

Sometimes, if I look up or

down too suddenly,

everything drops and my stomach gets swimmy and everything goes white.

It's not fun.

The Doctors did Some Tests.

They want to do Some More.

So, no / column this issue.

Sorry.
Sorry.
Sorry.

(Please don't

make
    me

go

down

the

stai rs.)

Ruth EJ Booth is a multiple award-winning writer based in Glasgow, Scotland. Their work can be found online at www.ruthbooth.com, on Twitter (@RuthEJBooth) and at Mastodon (@ruthejbooth@mastodon.scot)

The Tragedy
of Concrete

by Emma Levin

M odern life is complex. Mind-numbingly, bone-crunchingly, tooth-grindingly complex. In order to understand the anatomy of this present malaise, it could be argued that it is first necessary to dissect the past; to take the surgical steel scalpel of analysis to the soft and pliable dermis of events. For the seeds of the adversity which plagues the modern condition were first sown in the fertile mud of the twentieth century, and in the emergence of modern architecture. The story really begins, one could assert, in the 1920s, with Le Corbusier declaring that houses were "machines for living in" – primed to hobble their occupants or to launch them to success, contingent on the quality of the interior design and furnishings. His manifesto, because of course *everyone* had a manifesto in those days, outlined Five Points for a New Architecture. He called for roof gardens and horizontal windows, and for a total, unflinching absence of internal walls. While they were striking, his early houses were of questionable utility for the temperate climates in which they were installed – a contradiction expressed most succinctly in the paper *"Dear Monsieur Le Corbusier, It is still raining in our garage..."*

The incessant march of the twentieth century brought with it further trends. The curves of Bauhaus and Art Deco swept across

Art: Jon Stubbington

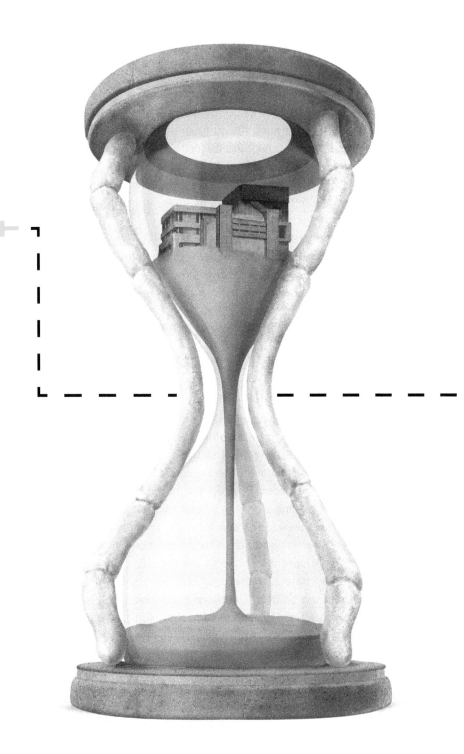

European countrysides like the railways which connected their growing suburbs. Myriad revivals – Mediterranean, Egyptian, and Spanish Colonial – forced courtyards and colonnades from the earth, with stuccoed miniature palaces and parodies of funerary monuments sitting grandly alongside tenement blocks, as if they had misread an invite, and come to the party in fancy dress. In the new Soviet Union, Futurism had graduated to Constructivism, El Lissitzky advancing from propaganda to print shops – kinetic confections of steel puncturing the Soviet skyline like daggers.

And then concrete arrived.

Concrete had, of course, existed for millennia. Ancient Egypt, Rome, and Greece had all left behind their own versions of concrete buildings – some even with volcanic ash and lime in the mix, an early innovation to let the material set underwater. But the true vector for concrete, in mid-twentieth century Europe, was Brutalism.

This style emerged in the shadow of war – in cities filled with "unplanned engineering works," the euphemistic name given to the waterlogged craters left behind by airborne ordinance. Concrete offered a quick, easy, and cost-effective way of throwing up replacement buildings. The aims of the Brutalists were lofty, both in principle and in practice. They sought to construct thoughtful, considered civic architecture, prioritising the public and the pedestrian over the motorcar and corporation, which were beginning slowly to encroach upon the city centre.

Brutalism was under attack from the moment it emerged. Indeed, the very name attached to the project is itself an insult, a corruption of the root, *béton brut,* the French for 'raw concrete.' Brutalism, as coined by the critic Reyner Banham, conjured up images of the bald, the stark, and the inhospitable. Spaces designed without concession to comfort; unfinished and crude.

In a way, one could argue that Brutalism was the last true radical architecture. A social movement as well as an architectural one, foregrounding communal spaces – of and for the community. If one adopted a cynical position, one could argue that the dereliction that was allowed to befall the Brutalist projects in the 1980s was as much an attack on the utopian ideal of social housing as it was on the built fabric of the tower blocks. Margaret Thatcher's government could be said – if one were a cynic – to have allowed the buildings to lapse into deliberate disrepair, and to gain a reputation of synonymity with dank corners of municipal buildings. Of oppressive, crumbling, inefficient bureaucracies, and of weird vestigial corridors, labyrinthine and useless.

The utopian appeal of concrete, reaching for a new and better future, also travelled to Japan. There, Metabolism reigned – concrete viewed not as dead and rigid, but as alive and flexible. Modular tower blocks allowed inhabitants to move the leaf of their life from one stem to another, like freshwater algae choosing to cling to another rock. Concrete roads expanded like roots, twisting over and under existing networks of railways.

Nowhere was concrete embraced more enthusiastically than in China in the twenty-first century. In the thirty-six months between the beginning of 2011 and the end of 2013, China poured more concrete than the United States had disgorged in the entirety of the twentieth century. Up sprang vast skyscrapers, complex networks of motorway flyovers, reservoirs, power stations, bus terminals, and shopping centres.

The concrete genie was well and truly out of the concrete bottle.

The fundamental problem with concrete is that it degrades over time. Well-made concrete – mixed precisely and maintained in ideal conditions – can last for about a hundred years. When concrete is prepared hastily or maintained in a hostile environment – in industrial regions beset by acid rain, or temperate altitudes where freeze-thaw occurs, the infill of water and expansion of ice like a thousand tiny knives working away at hairline cracks – its lifespan can be as short as fifty years. Although other architectural styles did emerge in the late twentieth century – the UK's rabbit hutch flats wrapped in flammable cladding, the solarpunk optimism of South East Asia, and the neo-baroque decadence of Dubai – concrete remained, by volume, the default material of the twenty first century.

The problem around the world, but for China especially, with all of the buildings completed in such a short window, was that the concrete was all going to degrade at roughly the same time. Collapse would occur suddenly and simultaneously. The fracture of all twenty-first century motorways at the same time was untenable. Accordingly, a solution was sought.

Many radical and imaginative proposals were put forward. The one that seemed, for a while, the frontrunner, was "self-healing" concrete; concrete containing alveoli filled with dormant bacteria and starch. The idea was that when hairline cracks began to form, water would penetrate through the fissures, the bacteria would rehydrate, come to life, and start eating the starch – excreting calcite, and sealing themselves back inside, like monks being bricked into monasteries in the time of Henry the Eighth.

The problem with this, though, was that it didn't fundamentally solve the issue of entropy. It was a palliative, offering a slight extension of the lifespan until all the starch was used up, or until the bacteria denatured beyond the point of resurrection. The innovation which really addressed the problem was discovered, like so many things are, by accident.

The biotech firms had been working for some time on the synthesis of artificial meat. They had focused on weaving delicate webs of actin and myosin for rich vegans, an expensive parody of flesh and morality. What changed everything was the accidental discovery that it was actually much easier to grow bone than to grow muscle. Strong, lightweight, and able to fuse in sections, bone was an almost ideal building material – a sponge, hardened by minerals. Sure, it required a blood supply, but this seemed a minor inconvenience for a material that promised not to degrade suddenly and catastrophically.

And so the era of the bone scaffold began.

The New Metabolists

The first architectural school to embrace bone as a building material were the New Metabolists. Based in Japan, they believed that organic building materials had significant potential – and had done ever since beams of oak were bent into lintels, hair was stirred into lime mortar, and wattle and daub were smeared over woven reeds.

The conditions in Japan were ideal for experimentation; the amount of work required to fix their creaking twentieth century rail network was daunting. To use traditional methods would be to render the entire system inoperable for a period of not months, but years – a feat both politically and practically indefensible. With a population that was both dwindling and ageing, there would in any case be a steep shortfall in the numbers of construction workers required to undertake such a monumental task. And so, in the rail network's time of need, the "New Metabolists" stepped into the phone box of necessity, ripping off their shirts and glasses to reveal the spandex of pragmatism and the cape of competence. They offered to encase the sinusoidal waves of the bullet train tracks in a healthy, vigorous bone scaffolding. And the plan was enthusiastically approved, with a pilot scheme in Kyoto.

Although it required considerably fewer workers, the project was still a gargantuan undertaking. Across the Kansai countryside, warehouse-nurseries played witness to a Lilliputian scene – workers bustling around the edges of vast growing frames, tiny in comparison to the monuments of flesh which were staked to the earth.

After the success of the Japanese experiment, the new material spread rapidly around the globe. As ever with architectural schools, there were regional variations. In the smouldering remains of the European Union, the bone was sculpted into parodies of classical forms – Doric, Ionic, and Corinthian columns implying a continuity with the traditions of yore. In East Asia, curved constructions participated in an uneasy dialogue with inorganic materials – finally achieving what Zaha Hadid had attempted in her lifetime, buildings which appeared as if poured rather than sculpted. And in the UK, that green and septic isle, The New Metabolism was spread predominantly by the architectural practice of Sir Arthur Mason. His manifesto – because, of course, they all had manifestos at this point – claimed that the true aim of "bioarchitecture" was the same as the guarantee voiced by Virgil and then stamped on the side of a pound coin. *Decus et tutamen* – as an ornament and a safeguard. This went down well with the conservative lot, who for some reason still venerated the classics.

Just as Brutalism was hampered by an unaffectionate label, so too The New Metabolism was cruelly nicknamed, in a way that came to stick like chewing gum matted into hair. Although it appeared subsequently in many anglophone nations, the British critic Lesley Brine was the first to use the word "wetware" – conjuring up images of the soft and the unsanitary. The name caught on around the world, except for in Germany, where *"die Lebenskunst"* (living craft) or *"Knochenstraßen"* (bone streets) were all part of a national plan of *"Aufbau"* – of building up. As with Brutalism before it, it is worth noting that the connotations of this colloquial name were shamelessly derogatory. Where "The New Metabolism" had overtones of dynamism, of adaptation, of resilience, and of invention, "wetware" conjured images of abattoir floors, slick with miscellaneous fluids.

And yet the name stuck.

Just as Brutalism had spread across the globe as a question of expediency – filling in the cracks left behind by high-impact explosives dropped from a height – so wetware oozed into the filigree of fractures left behind by the twentieth century's lack of foresight. In the rich breeding ground of optimism and myopia, wetware flourished.

In the UK, the technology was used predominantly on the network of ageing motorways. As a result of cost having been the driving principle behind the design of municipal infrastructure, there existed a lattice of concrete flyovers across the nation, hoisting arterial roads over suburbs like skirts above waves at the beach. Concrete had long been used to patch up the holes in the urban infrastructure, and as it reached the end of its natural lifespan, in high winds one could hear it groaning and clicking, the stresses rendered audible, and therefore unignorable.

Accordingly, vast joists of bone were grown up and around existing concrete, reinforcing the structures with great gleaming colonnades. The idea was that ribcages would support the beams – jointed to absorb the vibrations of the four-seater vehicles which were still common at the time, and giving the uncanny feeling that the roads were held up by a series of cupped hands, carefully carrying the driver to their destination while the concrete slowly reverted to sand, and trickled through their upturned fingers.

And so, while the science fiction visionaries of the twentieth century had imagined cyberpunk as *the flesh made metallic*, William Gibson writing about shiny cybernetic appendages and enhanced bionic eyes, the truth that came to pass was *the machine rendered in flesh*; strong and cheap. Of all the artists of the twentieth century, the screenwriter and director David Cronenberg had thrown his darts closest to the truth, with his throbbing visions of guns made of cartilage, chitinous typewriters, and palpitating, diseased games consoles.

At this point, it is worth revisiting the question of ideology. For the Brutalists, the core essence of the idea, the beating heart of the school (if one will forgive the crude metaphor) was that the public could – and should – be prioritised. For wetware, the tacit idea buried in the thorax of the project was that things could – and should – be made sustainable. Wetware imagined a world where obsolescence had not been baked-in. Where structures were not sustainable in the traditional sense, but rather *self-sustaining*. Conventional manufacturing methods had implied a mode of engagement with the world that began with a lit fuse – an internal clock ticking down from the minute that structures were erected, until they would need maintenance, require replacement, or collapse into the comfortable armchair of decay. Wetware was a process, rather than a product. And this was truly radical.

That is not to elide the fundamental truth that wetware took a huge amount of effort both to manufacture and to sustain. If tended carefully, the wetware could live indefinitely. But maintenance was extensive, expensive, and expansive, requiring the emergence of new industries and new infrastructure, dedicated solely to keeping the bones alive.

The Biology of Bridges

On paper, The New Metabolism had seemed to be a project of substitution; of swapping out concrete for bone. In reality, the task was far more complex. Bone, it transpired, had needs. And to fail to meet them would result in the irreversible death of the structure. Oxygen, calcium, and glucose had to be delivered constantly and consistently. The waste products of nitrogen and phosphorous had to be removed, swiftly and successfully. A vast network of pipes – functionally equivalent to arteries and veins – was constructed, with Teflon tubing swagged between posts like waterlogged bunting. Huge warehouses concealed the functions of survival in the suburbs. Behind the closed doors of aluminium sheds, industrial dialysis machines whirred, leeching contaminants from the artificial blood and returning it to circulation. In brownfield sites, among the carcasses of dead industry, the architects constructed vast artificial lungs. It was a fact commonly parroted that if you were to take every cell in a human lung and flatten them out, laying them side by side, they'd cover the area of a tennis court. For the purposes of keeping the bridges alive, many thousands of tennis courts were required. These "blood marshes", as they came to be known, housed neat snakes of silicon tubing, staked out in laps of the available area, exposing the artificial blood to the air as it passed through at dizzying speed. From the blood marshes, the fluid returned via pumping stations, the network of pipes which carried them back to the structures pulsing under the pressure. This distributed network of stations – blood marshes, dialysis sheds, pressure pumps, and monitoring huts – effectively turned the city into one vast superorganism, and all of its residents into enveloped endosymbionts.

It is worth briefly noting that the prominence of the pipe network in the UK was again a result of political will. In theory, the elements could have been buried beneath the pavement, like the pipes which dealt with water and waste. But in the UK, again, cost was so prevailing a factor in decision-making that it was considered viable for the pipes to throb in the sunlight.

Most people accepted the service network of infrastructure as inevitable and ignorable, and it was soon rendered invisible through exposure – in the same way that the Victorians soon ignored the manholes which hinted at Bazalgette's sewers, or the population of the 1930s was soon able to turn a blind eye to the National Grid's forest of pylons. Like boiling a frog, the concessions were introduced so gradually that at no point did they seem absurd or alarming.

That's not to say that there wasn't cultural resistance. As a profession, working on the wetware maintenance network was heavily stigmatised, the worst censure reserved for the "flesh gardeners" who patrolled the network, excising growths that needed to be -ectomied. The warehouse-nurseries for the new material also remained taboo. For although wetware was saving the crumbling cities, British society couldn't ignore the aesthetic echoes of the zombie films of the twenty-first century, the image of the outstretched hand grasping at the sun from cold loam.

And vocal detractors did remain.

The 2045 polemic article by Sir Anthony Gardener *"This city needs a DNR – all those who truly loved it are gone"* argued that, much like an elderly patient jammed into a pair of bellows against their will, the city and its occupants had not consented to these measures – and that the concessions to keep it alive were both cruel and unusual. In many ways, he suggested, the experiment of wetware was a lesson in the deviation between expectation and reality. The project had promised a return to strength. Overtones of rejuvenation and vigour. But the web of throbbing vessels which now wove through the urban fabric, like electrical cables across a film set, was disturbing. Their delicacy hinted at man's own fragility and mortality. And though the city had long been imagined through metaphors of vitality – described as thriving, or having a pulse – the actual physical manifestation of this symbolism was profoundly troubling.

Response to Sir Anthony in the architectural community was swift and decisive. Perhaps no essay was more widely-circulated (or loudly praised) than Dr Celia McMahon's *"Second Cyborg Manifesto"*. Dr McMahon proposed that "we have always smeared the Vaseline of retrospect on the lens of recall". That the urban, the city, the metropolis, has always been a messy affair. Squalid, in the classical sense – of dirt. If history, as they say, is written by the winners, then archaeology is written by the durable. We remember the Romans, Greeks, Minoans, and Egyptians as grand civilisations because of the monuments they have left behind. But only the finest buildings remain; we interpret their civilisations as splendid – that is, in the classical sense, filled with splendour – because it's only the jewels and the palaces which have withstood the clicking mandibles of time. On the basis of sheer quantity, our understanding of the Medieval should be underpinned by relics of the cess pit, the slum, and the compost heap. The narrative we are able to read is the one which was etched in almonries and bell towers. But it is not the one which actually happened.

Anyone with the faintest shred of awareness about them will recognise that quite apart from the aesthetic implications, the soft and widely-distributed nature of the wetware's service network made the made the system vulnerable. In theory, anyone could have taken a ladder and a pair of secateurs to the nearest pipe, and watched the contents disgorge onto the pavement until it reflected the sun. But in the same way that most people didn't take a bolt-cutter to their nearest telephone exchange, or a crowbar to their nearest manhole, the pipes remained unmolested.

The attack, when it came, was ideological.

The Anatomy of Conflict (and The Conflict of Anatomy)

For many years, the urge of biologists has been to classify, sorting lifeforms and phenomena into neat taxonomies, and inventing new words by concatenating long chains of Greek prefixes. Now that wetware had gained significant traction, and it was clear that it was here to stay, the biologists moved in; a sub-set of ecologists trying to work out precisely what the relationship between wetware and humanity might be called.

One school proposed that wetware was an 'epibiont,' living on the surface of the urban fabric in the same way that ivy girds an oak, or molluscs adhere themselves to the surface of a whale. In this conception, it was implicit that wetware had a degree of parasitism – humanity forming the substrate upon which it fed. Another school reversed this conception, arguing that it was humanity living on the surface of wetware, a mutualistic exchange much like clownfish cowering in the fronds of an anemone. Still others proposed that wetware was a textbook case of 'endosymbiosis,' a relationship in which one creature physically housed the other, in a grotesque parody of a Russian doll. Much like the bacteria that lounged in the human colon, they suggested that humanity now operated in the warm embrace of the artificial bone.

None of these depictions were considered flattering to humanity.

Debates around symbiosis and mankind had raged before – with a surprisingly heated argument over whether humans had domesticated wheat, or whether wheat had domesticated humans. Compelling arguments existed, explaining that the transition from nomadic to agrarian social arrangements, where almost all waking hours were spent in careful stewardship of the crop, looked very much on paper like humans were in service to the grain. These battles, though, were purely intellectual – confined to the pages of textbooks, and the context of the Holocene. The arguments over the classification of wetware, however, felt raw. They were splashed across the comment pages of newspapers like vomit across flagstones. When all the facts were written down, the relationship did seem uncertain. It was true that a huge amount of enterprise and capital were dedicated to keeping the bones alive. Were the bones propping up the city, or was the city now in service to the bones? The jury was very much out.

In discussions of science and technology, of art and architecture and history, there is a tendency for texts to lapse into hagiography. The idea persists that the flailing tentacles of progress tear chunks off the corpse of the present, and guide them to the toothless beak of the future, only under the impetus provided by exceptional individuals, rather than incrementally and through the collective innovation of society. While this tendency towards sycophantic reverence is unhelpful in the broad sense, it must be acknowledged that is impossible to unpick the events of 2073 without reference to the figure of Katy Birnam.

Sociologists working on the roll-out of wetware had assumed that the most likely source of threat to the system would come from war – with anxiety crystallising around vulnerability to external agents. For many years, the dominant direction of warfare had been shifting, with a tendency to attack infrastructure rather than population. (Because, as it turned out, there was nothing more effective at twisting the hearts and minds of a populace against their stubborn regime like turning off the internet and water.) Killing individual citizens at random felt both archaic and ethically questionable. The idea of poisoning infrastructure, however, of developing bioweapons which gave bridges rickets or diseases that would infiltrate the bone, stripping mineral from the matrix, and reverting it back to sponge, showed significant promise. And that was before they considered the idea of zoonotic diseases. The anxiety that you could catch something off your morning commute would be a powerful fear, and a powerful deterrent to using the network.

Instead, it was Katy Birnam, and a fear of ecological dominance, which proved instrumental in the downfall of wetware. In the history of the UK, the single-issue political parties which have performed appreciably at the polls have always been those which were driven by fear. Fear of immigration. Fear of irrelevance. Fear of impotence. All drove conversations in wider politics as a result of unexpected electoral success. Katy Birnam stood for election as Mayor of London on the platform that wetware was unnatural and should not be indulged. Her rhetoric reflected that fragile alloy of ego and insecurity which said that the way to demonstrate dominion over an entity is to maltreat it. Not for the first time, the citizens of the UK could only watch as their infrastructure was dismantled not by hostility or misfortune, but through political folly.

In London, expenditure on maintenance was halved, with

feedstuffs substituted for lower and lower quality. In a matter of months, the Blackwall Tunnel succumbed to atrophy. It began visibly to fall apart – changing colour, desiccating, and presenting a flaccid impersonation of its former self, like an ageing athlete viewed as a pundit after twenty years out of the spotlight. In a number of weeks, it became apparent that the tunnel was dead. The problem with the deceased tunnel, quite apart from its diminished structural integrity, was the smell. The unignorable stench of decay, which prompted the same discomfort felt at visiting an old-age home, an ingrained and instinctive distaste for necrosis. Katy Birnam took to the television, pronouncing the death a resounding indictment of the wetware system (and completely eliding her own role in the event).

The problem, though, remained. In the same way that stone buildings leave behind durable ruins, and brownfield sites stain the earth with the toxic and the flammable, the bones needed a method of disposal.

The Necessity of Disposal

A competition was held to devise an appropriate method of clearance – the problem being a novel challenge which required novel solutions. One group of engineers proposed harvesting the dead bones and grinding them up to fine meal to re-use the calcium, much as one might give a cuttlefish bone to a budgerigar, feeding it back into the system. Though economically frugal, the proposal was dismissed on the basis of biosecurity, of the novel, transmissible diseases that might emerge – lessons learned from the prions of BSE. With a prevailing emphasis on green technologies, one group proposed bio-disposal. In 2002, an expedition of marine scientists has discovered a species of worm which feasted on the sunken bones of whales. These 'ossivores' or 'bone eaters' were capable of mindlessly devouring the vast, unwanted masses of calcium and collagen. In lifecycle, they could be considered analogous to dandelions – growing fast, reproducing furiously, and casting their eggs to the mercy of currents, the strategy of the weed. The worms were to be contained in aquariums, which were to be concealed underground – portions of dead bridge delivered at intervals. (A 'solution' which, in the long term, created as many problems as it solved).

It is worth noting here that so often in the history of human progress, energy is spent making increasingly onerous accommodations to preserve a system which had never been fit for purpose. To have suggested a vast system of carnivorous vermiculture, distributed throughout urban centres like raisins in a pudding or cat pictures on a hard-drive, would have at one point seemed both absurd and alarming. But buildings have always demanded gross amounts of surreal maintenance. If one considers the life cycle of thatch, the dangerous profession of the chimney sweep, or the dangling window cleaner suctioned to the side of the skyscraper like a remora, the vermiculture of the late 2070s may not seem so outlandish. As Katy Birnam wrote in her re-election manifesto, *"the altar of tomorrow is slick with the blood of yesterday, and we may not recognise the face of the present when we look in the mirror."* Admittedly, she was writing this as an invective, a denouncement and condemnation of The New Metabolism, but the critique cuts both ways. The present is unthinkable to the past because so much of our decision-making is driven by the fear of imagined faults, rather than the actual shortcomings rendered in metal and bone. Tabloid coverage of the ossivorous worms focused on the potential risk to human life, the narratives of contagion etched into the gelid exo-brain of culture, stressing the fatuity of keeping something bone-eating in proximity to our own delicious bones. But the genuine threat, bubbling under the surface like resentment in a marriage, was the fear that wetware would outlive us. Around the globe, regimes of neo-austerity emerged, following the template that Birnam pioneered, of starving the wetware, and then decrying its weakened state as an admission of failure. In Germany, projects emerged under the banner of The New Bauhaus, reaching again for a unison of *Disziplinen,* a *Gesamtkunstwerk* embracing the industrial and the aesthetic simultaneously. As the bone decayed, it was encased in steel – in the same way that teeth had been wired into metal tracks in twentieth century orthodontics. Like the strata of lino on a cheaply-renovated kitchen floor, or the lamination of wallpapers on tenement walls, concrete was doubly-wrapped; encased first in bone, and then circumscribed by steel.

While some did protest the sabotage of the wetware, most stood by and watched it happen, silent and complicit.

In Conclusion

The convention within accounts of architecture is for a piece of writing to chart the lifecycle of a trend – to follow the rise and fall and revival of a particular style or school. To highlight the lessons learned and insights gained, and to end on some sort of spectacular metaphor. So far, we have considered the fall of concrete and the rise of bone, the downward inflection of the curve starting to hint at the beginning of the end (or perhaps, more accurately, the end of the beginning).

For it is tempting, in prose, to construct an argument and a narrative which appears watertight. To ask "how did the situation resolve?" and then immediately to provide an answer. I will not insult you with such gross simplification. The truth of the matter is that there was never resolution and there will never be any resolution to the trajectory of wetware. Because history is just a series of moments compressed into the hopper of an industrial grinder, and then extruded into the sausages of narrative. In the same way that film is merely a flickering sequence of images that the limitations of our brains read as motion, so too is the complexity of the world squashed by our ape-like need to identify patterns. The rudderless, aimless, *stochastic* meandering of event and consequence cannot be grasped by our mammalian minds. And so we must superimpose abstract nouns onto the relentless stream of developments, labelling things tragedies or victories in order to render them comprehensible and meaningful.

It is a truth widely acknowledged that the enemy of progress is not inertia but nostalgia. That the enemy of innovation is not tradition, but fear. That emotional arguments carry weight beyond the numerical and rational. And that Exceptionalism

– the idea that humanity stands above other species on a pedestal of intellect, aptitude, and arrogance, underpins the majority of enterprise. Was wetware doomed from the start? Who decides whether its memory should be deified or defiled?

As I sit here in the cannibalised corpse of the past, writing with the aggregate of pedantry and ego that is so often incubated in the academy, the image that strikes me is that of Ozymandias, of monuments crumbling with sand as a witness, bare and impassive. I suspect the idea that I should leave you with is that our architecture is a reflection of our society. That the assumption of improvement and progress is a projection of what we would like to see in ourselves. It is with no joy that I regret to inform you that there are only two certainties in life; that any truly radical architecture will be sabotaged, and that politicians will devote energy not to fixing the problem, but to wondering whether it would be worse to appear ignorant of the situation, or powerless to fix it.

Emma Levin's writing has appeared in magazines (e.g. **Popshot**), anthologies (e.g. **The Best of British Science Fiction** 2019, 2021), online (e.g. **Daily Science Fiction**), and in many recycling bins. She sometimes writes for videogames and for radio, and can be found online at: emmalevinwrites.com

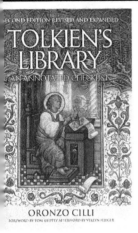
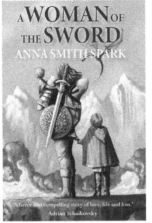

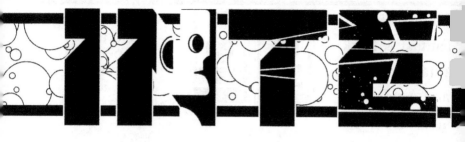

Q&A with
Ian Whates
of NewCon Press

Teika Marija Smits
asks the questions

Teika Marija Smits: *NewCon Press came into being back in 2006 with the publication of its first title,* Time Pieces. *When you first published that anthology, did you ever think you'd go on to publish 100+ titles (and counting!)?*

Ian Whates: Not at all. I always say that NewCon was founded by accident, and that's true. *Time Pieces* was intended as a one-off, released to cover the debt left by a convention that lost money. Once completed, I held the book in my hand and thought "I did this! I can do it again," completely forgetting the missteps and traumas along the way. Even then, the plan was to publish the occasional book to run alongside my writing career. By the end of the third year we had released five titles, little imagining that by the end of our 16th the total would reach 185.

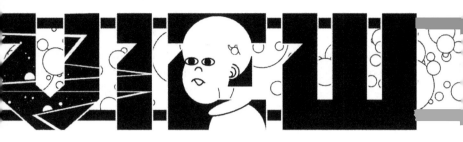

You currently pretty much run NewCon Press singlehandedly. How on earth do you manage to achieve so much, and have you recently thought, 'Crumbs, I need to outsource some of this work!'?

There are times when I would love to outsource and, indeed, have done so in a minor way from time to time. But the sad truth is we don't make sufficient money to justify employing someone on a regular basis, even part-time. My far better half, Helen, looks after the dispatching of customer orders and keeps an eye on stock levels, while I cover pretty much everything else. It leaves us vulnerable in the event of forced absence for whatever reason, but there we are. As for how... I simply prioritise the most urgent task and, when that's done, move onto the next. (There is more pleasure involved than that suggests, honest!)

NewCon Press publishes in a variety of genres, namely: science fiction, fantasy, dark fantasy and horror. You also publish anthologies, short story collections, novellas and novels. And, unusually for a smallish indie press, you also publish books in various formats: signed limited hardbacks, paperbacks and ebooks via Amazon. What are the pros to this kind of diversity?

I publish what I would like to read, so I suppose the variety is an indication of my own taste. I grew up reading copious amounts of SF and nearly as much fantasy, but far less horror, and that's reflected in our list. I've always liked signed limited editions, and the first two NewCon titles were purely that, but economics dictate that we also produce more affordable paperback editions to make the business sustainable, so producing both has become the norm.

What makes you want to publish a manuscript?

That's difficult to quantify. (And I would save myself so much time if I could.) The quality of the writing is a big factor, but telling an engaging story is just as vital. Having something original to say is always a big draw, even if it's just putting a fresh twist on the familiar. Essentially, it comes down to whether I would invest my own money to read this. If the answer is 'yes', then the author's in with a good chance.

Which brings me nicely on to my next question: how do you go about commissioning books for NewCon?

In all honesty, I rarely do because I haven't needed to (touch wood). Despite being officially closed to submissions, we receive so many approaches on spec that I've more than enough material to consider. The only time I actively approach anyone is for a specific project; either stories for an anthology or a series of books which I believe a given author would be ideal for.

You work with a number of superb illustrators for your covers. How do you match an author's book to an artist?

Usually, that's pretty straightforward. It's a privilege to work with such an array of fantastic artists, and when I read a manuscript it's often apparent who to approach first, whose style I think would best capture the book. Sometimes that artist is unavailable for whatever reason, so I'll have a rethink, but most of the time it works out.

What has been one of your greatest challenges while running the press? And your greatest successes?

Greatest challenge: sticking with it through the loss-making early years.

Greatest successes: many. Seeing a book by an unknown author I have faith in succeed. Seeing a novel we published picked up by a major publisher. Winning several BSFA and British Fantasy Awards. Seeing NewCon titles feature on the Arthur C. Clarke Award shortlist for the past two years running. Winning an award for being the 'best genre publisher' in Europe. Working long into the night for a fortnight to rush out an anthology to help provide PPE for frontline staff during the very first lockdown, and seeing it raise £3,500.

Any hard-won wisdom (about life or publishing!) that you'd like to pass on?

Huh! I make no claims of 'wisdom', leaving such things to those with a far greater belief in the worth of their own opinions than I possess. I've made some inspired choices and I've made mistakes (and it's not always immediately obvious which is which). I've learned new skills and shied away from learning others due to lack of time and/or inclination. I suspect I've made enemies but hope I've made far more friends. And that's the most important thing: both in work and in life, surround yourself with people you care about and whom you can rely on, as they can rely on you.

As a former publisher myself (and now editor-at-large) I know it's hard to single out any one title as being a 'favourite', but if there were one NewCon book that we should all go out and buy right now, which would it be?

In all honesty, no. I believe in everything we publish, and the books are too varied to single out one as 'representative'. An anthology is always a good way to sample a variety of authors and discover those you might want to read more by. If you want an indication of my own taste and whether NewCon's roster might be for you, perhaps *London Centric* or *2001: An Odyssey in Words* for SF, *Legends* for fantasy, but even these will oWnly reveal a single facet of a far more diverse whole.

Lastly... a pint of real ale or a G&T...?!

Either/both (though not in the same glass), depending on the circumstances.

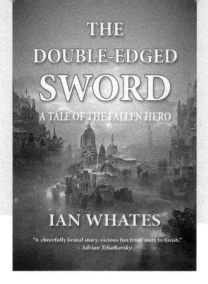

"A cheerfully brutal story, vicious fun from start to finish."
– Adrian Tchaikovsky

The Double-Edged Sword

Ian Whates

Excerpt from Chapter 1: Not a Moment to Swoon

"Was Gerard really as magnificent as they say?"

I suppressed a groan. Oh well, he was paying. "Gerard was certainly magnificent to look at," I conceded. "Tall, bronzed, well-muscled with golden hair…"

"A great, great hero."

I snorted, "Yeah, right. He was awkward with a bow, a passably good swordsman and a hopeless strategist – some hero."

Predictably, that surprised him. The Gerard I'd just described was at odds with the one painted by popular myth in every way, which was a tremendous tribute to the man's true genius: the ability to manipulate his own public image.

"Awkward…? *Passable*? Why did the rest of you follow him, in that case?"

Why indeed? No mystery really; the reasons were obvious once you took the trouble to look at them. "He had the rep," I said.

Gerard wasn't a man who ever felt the need to play down his notoriety – quite the opposite, in fact: he revelled in it, *relished* it, and we all benefited as a result.

"Don't get me wrong," I continued, "he wasn't stupid. He surrounded himself with people who were experts at the things he wasn't. I was a miles better swordsman, for example, and so was Alvin. Cedric was the best archer I've ever seen and Tam, who joined us after Cedric was killed at Arden Falls, wasn't far behind. Jaeko was a master at planning and strategy and old Sirus had a few tricks that had to be seen to be believed. Claimed they were sorcery and they probably were, if you give credence to that sort of thing. Each and every one of us had our uses.

"Thing was, by following Gerard we got all the plum jobs and the big rewards – the sort that none of us would ever have had a sniff at on our own. He had the reputation, you see, he was 'The Hero.' Only ever one man to call on in a crisis: Gerard."

"But surely there must have been *something* special about him," the youth insisted. "After all, he must have won that reputation somehow in the first place."

"Oh yes," I assured him, "there was something special about him all right. His power over women."

"His fabled charm."

"No," I shook my head, "it was more than that. It was like a bewitchment, a spell if you will, which he could turn on and off just like that," I snapped my fingers. "I've seen it happen. One minute we'd be getting nowhere with some stuck-up lady this or countess that, with her not giving an inch on payment rates or terms, then suddenly she would stop in mid-sentence, forget what she'd been saying and go weak at the knees. After that she'd be putty in his hands. It was quite something."

"You really believe that? You think it was some sort of magical power?"

I shrugged and muttered, "Fairy moans."

"Pardon?"

"Oh, just something Sirus told me once. He said he reckoned it was all down to fairy moans. Maybe he was right, I never did know much about sorcery. Maybe Gerard was able to summon the voices of fairies that only women could hear, bewitching them." I shrugged, "Used to listen hard whenever I knew he was doing it… never heard any fairies though, moaning or otherwise.

"Sirus would just laugh when I told him and say I was doing it wrong, that I should have been listening with my nose, but he always was a funny old coot."

"Incredible." The lad was well and truly hooked.

"Thirsty work, this story telling," I glanced meaningfully at my now empty tankard.

"Oh… I'm sorry," he stood up. "Allow me."

With pleasure.

Ale replenished, I set about telling him what had happened, describing briefly how we had risen to prominence after a series of successful jobs, each of which led to the next one, slightly more significant than the last and correspondingly more rewarding.

Then came the big one. The council of Trilmouth approached us and asked for our help. This was major league at last, what we had been working towards. Trilmouth was one of the top trading cities. If we could make ourselves useful to them, indispensable even, then we really had cracked it.

It emerged that the Crystal of Relf had been stolen. Even I had heard of that hallowed chunk of glass. Bequeathed to the city by its founder, the 'sorcerer' King Relf, it was said to contain great power. Many believed that Trilmouth owed its success and pre-eminence entirely to the mystical properties of the crystal. However real or imagined those powers might be, the council felt the city's influence would wane without it.

To make matters worse, it had been stolen by one of their own number following a disagreement. Said to be a sorceress herself, the Lady Margeaut had snatched the crystal and fled to her castle hideaway in the mountains above the city. The council were now uncertain of whom among their own troops and contacts were to be trusted, so they turned to us.

They offered a reward larger than everything we had earned to date combined – enough that each of us could retire in reasonable comfort, if we chose to.

I described in slightly greater detail what happened on the fateful day itself – how we tricked our way into the castle, how we had penetrated deep within before being discovered and then had to fight our way after that. Swordplay in a confined space is a great leveller and as we made our way upward in pursuit of a fleetingly glimpsed woman who stayed tantalisingly out of reach, every step demanded payment in sweat and blood. Not much of it our blood, thankfully. We were good; very good.

She fled to the very roof of the highest tower and it was there that we finally cornered her.

"It was a frozen tableau," I explained, milking it, aware that he was hanging on my every word. "The lady Margeaut poised on the brink of the parapet, glorious in silk and velvet, illuminated by moonlight and sputtering torches, golden hair flowing in the wind, which whipped her dress about like some half-furled banner. Her hand was held out, suspending the precious orb over the void.

"Tam was there, staring down the shaft of an arrow pointed at her heart; me and Alvin flanked him, with swords drawn, wondering if we dared inch any closer, whilst Jeanty stood off to one side, debating whether any of his acrobatics would enable him to catch the crystal if she did drop it…

"And at the centre stood Gerard. Magnificent, Golden Gerard. The voice of reason, telling her that it was finished, insisting that if she would just step away from the edge no harm would befall her, that he personally guaranteed her safety if she would just hand over the crystal. It was working too. She was weakening, starting to discuss terms. Any fool could see that she was on the point of yielding, that she was about to give up… Well, any fool but one, apparently. Another moment and it would have been job done, but do you know what the stupid oaf did then? What the great Golden Buffoon just had to go and do?"

My audience shook his head, enthralled.

"He turned on his much-vaunted *charm*, that's what. It wasn't happening quickly enough for our Gerard, oh no. Mere words were too slow, so he had to do it the easy way, the dumb ox!" I paused, shaking with fury even now, after all these years.

"And?" I was prompted.

"She swooned. Literally collapsed. You could see the exact instant when Gerard's power hit her. One minute she stood there, beautiful and defiant, the next she just crumpled, lost her balance and toppled right over the edge, with all of us lunging to try and catch her. Jeanty even managed to grab hold of a corner of her dress, but it tore as she fell and he was left holding no more than a tatter of silk." I stopped speaking, seeing it all again, unable to go on for the moment. "Biggest purse of our lives and he had to go and do that!" I muttered at length.

"Is that when you hit him?"

I nodded, "Smack on his golden bloody chin."

"None of this ever came out," he said breathlessly.

"Of course not. Gerard was still the meal ticket after all, so the others all got together and decided to salvage what they could. Thus the official story emerged – about how we had fought valiantly through the castle to confront the evil sorceress on the roof of its highest tower, from whence she flung herself to her doom, taking the crystal with her rather than surrender it to its rightful custodians."

"But you refused to go along with that story?"

"Too true. I'm a man of principle, you see. I'd had more than enough of the Golden Gorilla and his posturing by then. Besides which," I felt obliged to concede, "that punch broke his jaw, so he wasn't too keen on having me around any more."

"Which is why you were thrown in jail."

"Yup, that's about the size of it. For assaulting the great *Hero*." I drained my tankard. "Well, there you have it – the real story of what went on. Thanks for the drinks." I went to rise. "All such a long time ago," I muttered. "The only thing I still have from those days is the ornamental dagger Gerard gave me that time when I saved his life. Of course, we were on better terms back then."

"Can I see it?" he said at once.

"The knife? Sorry, I haven't got it with me, it's back at my room."

"Oh." Obvious disappointment.

"…which isn't really that far – just around the corner, in fact, if you'd care to come back and see it."

"Would you mind?"

I shrugged, "I was going there anyway."

So we left together, with him still talking, still asking questions, which I answered in unhelpful monosyllables, my mind on other things.

It was dark already – the evenings were drawing in. As we stepped from the smoky warmth of the inn, the night greeted us with a cold slap to the cheeks. I led him through a narrow side street, badly lit, little more than an alley really.

His questions turned to the subject of the dagger. "Where did it come from exactly?"

"I'm not sure, *exactly* … One of his lady friends, no doubt – a token of undying love from some gentlewoman or other."

"Why have you kept it all this time?"

"Oh, it comes in useful." It really was dark here. We seemed to be the only two people out at this late hour.

"It can be used, then? It's a real knife, I mean, not just an ornament?"

"Oh no, it's perfectly serviceable," I assured him. "Here, let me show you."

With one fluid movement, I drew the knife from my belt, stepped in towards him and drove it deep into his belly, my free hand covering his mouth. In the dim light I could barely make out the look of disbelief and shock that froze his features. He had just started a low gasping moan when I drew the blade across his throat, silencing him forever.

He would have fallen then but for my supporting arm. I lowered him to rest in a sitting position against the wall. A quick glance round to make sure no one had seen anything, then I slipped a hand into his coat and relieved him of the bulging purse which had caught my attention when he first bought me a drink.

"You didn't stand a chance," I told his sightless eyes. "If not me, it would have been someone else." In truth, it was a miracle he had survived this long. His sort of naïvety came with a very short shelf-life.

I pocketed the purse, which felt satisfyingly heavy, then cleaned and did the same with the knife. "Sorry kid, but there's not much work around for retired heroes these days and I have to make a living somehow."

I stood, composed myself and strolled away, humming a half-remembered tune that Jimmy the Minstrel used to play around the camp fire. Gerard would invariably lead the singing with gusto. He had a decent voice, come to think of it.

Those were the days.

NewCon Press, 09/01/2023

£9.99 (Paperback) I £19.99 (Signed Hardback, Ltd. Ed.)

Pages: 80 pp. I ISBN: 978-1-914953-41-5

SHORELINE
OF INFINITY

Shoreline of Infinity is based in Edinburgh, Scotland, and began life in 2015.

Shoreline of Infinity Science Fiction Magazine is a print and digital magazine published quarterly in PDF ePub and Kindle formats. It features new short stories, poetry, art, review and articles.

But there's more – we run regular live science fiction events called Event Horizon, with a whole mix of science fiction related entertainments such as story and poetry readings, author talks, music, drama, short films – we've even had sword fighting.

We also publish a range of scienc fiction related books; take a look at our collection at the Shoreline Shop You can also pick up back copies of all of our issues. Details on our website ...

www.shorelineofinfinity.com

Also on social media. Links:
https://linktr.ee/shorelineofinfinity

TONER '17

Ingram Content Group UK Ltd.
Milton Keynes UK
UKHW022032080323
418264UK00011B/640